"One of the most truthful, painfu..."
—JOSEPH BRUCHAC

"*The Lesser Blessed* charts new territory on the literary map, and for this we must be thankful." —THE VANCOUVER SUN

"Van Camp penetrates the lives of his characters with compassion and empathy that transcends the fights, drugs, music and sex that characterize the stereotypical high school experience." —BOOKS IN CANADA

"Van Camp writes with a real honest connection. It's that honesty that makes his first novel such an achievement." —ABORIGINAL VOICES

"[Van Camp] does not stumble over nostalgia or romanticism or careless diction. He loves words 'his own, his Nation's, rock and roll's' and slips perfect ones into atrociously profane and perfect sentences.... Van Camp captures the hilarious pitch and putt of adolescent dialogue." —MALAHAT REVIEW

"*The Lesser Blessed* seems like a novel for adults, but one that might be both accessible and of interest to adolescent readers, who might well be especially attracted to its gritty subject matter and realistic representation of language and point of view..." —LETTERS IN CANADA

"Van Camp's novel introduces a new terrain and language that nonetheless has roots in the fiction of Momaday and Leslie Marmon Silko and James Welch, while simultaneously exploring the same subject matter as the contemporary stories of Sherman Alexie, Adrian Louis, and Lorne Simon...*The Lesser Blessed* is also a harbinger of a sophisticated Arctic Literature, and of a bold new direction for contemporary Native Literature." —GEARY HOBSON

20TH ANNIVERSARY SPECIAL EDITION

THE LESSER BLESSED

RICHARD VAN CAMP

Douglas & McIntyre

This book is dedicated to the memory of Lorne Joseph Simon,
author of *Stone and Switches* (1960-1994)

I remember...

Douglas and McIntyre (2013) Ltd.
PO Box 219, Madeira Park, BC VON 2HO
www.douglas-mcintyre.com

Cover design by Diane Robertson
Background cover photo from the film *The Lesser Blessed* (2012); image courtesy Entertainment One. Fire image by da-kuk/iStock.
Typesetting by Brianna Cerkiewicz
Printed and bound in Canada
Distributed in the US by Publishers Group West

Douglas and McIntyre (2013) Ltd. acknowledges the support of the Canada Council for the Arts, which last year invested $157 million to bring the arts to Canadians throughout the country. We also gratefully acknowledge financial support from the Government of Canada through the Canada Book Fund and from the Province of British Columbia through the BC Arts Council and the Book Publishing Tax Credit.

Canada Council   Conseil des arts
for the Arts   du Canada

BRITISH COLUMBIA
ARTS COUNCIL
An agency of the Province of British Columbia

Canadä

Cataloguing data available from Library and Archives Canada
ISBN 978-1-77162-113-7 (paper)
ISBN 978-1-77162-114-4 (ebook)

"Where Are You Tonight?" was originally published in *Prairie Fire* and included in *Night Moves*, Enfield & Wizenty, 2015. Reprinted with permission.

"How I Saved Christmas" was originally published in *Angel Wing Splash Pattern* published by Kegedonce Press, Cape Croker, Ontario. Reprinted with permission.

Contents

Introduction

DANET'E! HELLO!

Welcome to the Twentieth Anniversary Omnibus and Extenda-Mix Edition of *The Lesser Blessed*!

Twenty years! Twenty years. Twen-tee years!! I know where the time has gone but twenty years, baby!!

I remember the day I held my author's copy of *The Lesser Blessed* in my hands. 1996. Victoria student housing. Rain.

There were 117 pages of Larry Sole's confession. There were the last five years of my focus, sweet love, embarrassment and excitement. There it was and I couldn't take it back: I had fired an arrow of flaming light into the world and I had no idea who it would find. I was terrified.

I was in my third year at the University of Victoria where I was studying Creative Writing with some of Canada's greatest writers, and I was a long way from home: Fort Smith, NWT. I had no idea that I'd be the first member of the Tlicho Dene to ever write a novel; I had no idea that I'd be the first person from Fort Smith to ever write a novel. All I knew is, growing up in Fort Smith, I'd always loved to read: S.E. Hinton, Pat Conroy, Stephen King, Richard Brautigan, *The Warlord* (Mike Grell's comic), *Heavy Metal* magazine, *Epic* magazine. And I had always loved music: Platinum Blonde, Iron Maiden, My Bloody Valentine, The Cure, The Smiths, The Mission UK, The Sisters of Mercy and Fields of the Nephilim. I could get lost in music and, thankfully, I've never lost this gift. You'll see in the Acknowledgements in all of my books that I thank every artist or musician who helps me hone my writing.

Re-reading the novel for the first time in over 18 years, and going through old journals, I was reminded that, originally, *The*

Lesser Blessed was going to be called *Me and Johnny.* But after diving into the lyrics of the Fields of the Nephilim song "Celebrate," I could feel the mood and tone of the novel. I could sniff it. So I changed it to capture a title that was perfect for one of the first novels honouring second-generation residential school survivors. There's a reason Larry's dad speaks French when he molests him. Larry's story is so dark, so brutal, so raw, so real, but ultimately a story of hope and resilience and how love can save lives. Would I change a word after all this time? No. It's done. It's out. It's free. And that's why I was able to write baby books and books for children and use satire and self-deprecation to get everyone laughing. I had healed so many deep wounds and let so much pain go through Larry.

Growing up in Fort Smith and through all my reading, I had a sense that no one was sharing my story: no one was writing about having grandparents who were medicine people; no one was writing about driving your Ski-Doo to high school and then racing out past the highway to watch your brother check his snares before heading home to watch *Degrassi Junior High* on CBC; no one was talking about having spaghetti and meatballs with the meat being either caribou or buffalo.

The best piece of writing advice I've ever heard is, "Write something you'd like to read." So I started *The Lesser Blessed* when I was 19. I don't think it hit me that I was working on a novel. I just knew that Larry Sole was after me in whispers and belly laughs, secrets and sighs. And he was with me for five years.

Carolyn Swayze, bless you for reading it and thank you for showing it to Douglas & McIntyre, who bought it soon after reading it. Bless you, Barbara Pulling, for being the best editor for Larry's story. To the late Tim Atherton, mahsi cho for giving us the perfect cover for our first edition.

The smartest thing I ever did with my writing was invent a

community called Fort Simmer: it's an amalgamation of Fort Smith, Hay River and Behchoko, NWT. Since it's a fictional community, readers, family and friends were able to let their guards down and enjoy a story about the North.

In all the years I wrote the novel, it never occurred to me that I was writing a life story of a cousin of mine who ended his own young life, far too young and far too soon. I won't get into it but this novel is how I wish my cousin's life could have been.

Writing and publishing the novel also gave me the confidence to keep going: my Fort Simmer stories can be read in my short story collections, *Angel Wing Splash Pattern*, *The Moon of Letting Go*, *Godless but Loyal to Heaven* and *Night Moves*. You can also see Fort Simmer in my graphic novel *The Blue Raven* and my comic book *Kiss Me Deadly*. And you can read more from Darcy after the novel and the movie in a novel of his own in the short story "Whistle."

This new edition of the book includes two more stories with the same characters from *The Lesser Blessed*. You can read part two of *The Lesser Blessed* in "How I Saved Christmas," featured here for the first time outside of *Angel Wing Splash Pattern*. Mahsi cho to the late Duncan MacPherson and his family, who inspired this story. You can also follow Larry, Juliet, Darcy and Kevin through another evening in Fort Simmer in "Where Are You Tonight?", a story originally published in *Night Moves*. I wrote this story for the cast of *The Lesser Blessed* film so they could have more time with the characters. I'm in awe of everyone who brought the characters to life on the big screen.

I would like to acknowledge Anita Doron, who wrote to me years ago asking if I'd let her turn Larry's story into a feature film with First Generation Films. Thank God I said yes. Anita, I wouldn't change a thing about your adaptation of the novel. It's perfect. Christina Piovesan and Alex Lalonde, thank you for never giving up during the seven years it took to make our movie.

Joel Nathan Evans, mahsi cho for being the best Larry Sole for the adaptation, and mahsi cho to Tamara Podemski, Benjamin Bratt, Kiowa Gordon, Chloe Rose and Adam Butcher for being the perfect Verna, Jed, Johnny Beck, Juliet Hope and Darcy McMannus.

One of my prized possessions from the first twenty years of touring *The Lesser Blessed* is a CD a young student gave me years ago in Kelowna. I wish I could remember her name. She'd burned me a CD of *The Lesser Blessed*'s soundtrack. Here it is: the intro to Van Halen's "1984;" AC/DC's "Highway to Hell" and "Back in Black;" Billy Idol's "Mony Mony;" Bruce Springsteen's "Dancing in the Dark;" Tommy James and the Shondells' "Crimson and Clover;" Heart's "Crazy on You;" Iron Maiden's "Run to the Hills," "The Loneliness of the Long Distance Runner" and "Powerslave;" Judas Priest's "Turbo Lover;" Night Ranger's "Sister Christian;" The Cult's "She Sells Sanctuary;" The Outfield's "Talk to Me" and Journey's "Midnight Train."

I have a framed poster of the movie, which premiered at the Toronto International Film Festival at 4 pm on September 9, 2012 (my whole family was there!), and I have the official embroidered *Lesser Blessed* gloves, which were given out to everyone on set while shooting in Sudbury and Atikameksheng Anishnawbek, ON. I have the official and final screenplay, the visual reference book (which I treasure), and I took portraits of all of the actors in character. I'm proud that I was able to work with the revered German author Ulrich Plenzdorf on the German translation of the novel for Ravensburger, and I am grateful that I was able to work on a French translation with Gaia Editions' Nathalie Mège as my translator.

I would like to dedicate the twentieth edition of *The Lesser Blessed* to my mom, Rosa Wah-shee; to my dad, Roger Brunt; and to my father, Jack Van Camp. My brothers, Roger, James and Johnny, I want to dedicate this twentieth edition to you, too. As well, I'd like to honour my wife, Keavy Martin, and our son, Edzazii. My wife, my son, I am so proud to share this 20th anniversary with you. As well, I could not have written the novel without the charm and gorgeous spirit of Fort Smith: her land, her people, her magic.

Mahsi cho to everyone who ever came out to a reading or invited me on a tour. I've been able to travel to so many parts of the world sharing stories from the North. I'm proud of this. I am grateful to every professor and teacher who taught the novel. Mahsi cho.

Twenty books in twenty years on the twentieth anniversary of *The Lesser Blessed*. Now how cool is that?

I'm just so grateful to Larry Sole for calling my name all those years ago. Larry, bless you. I am so grateful to have known and to honour you.

Here's to more writing and more stories.

Mahsi cho, everyone!

Richard Van Camp
Tlicho Dene from Fort Smith, NWT
November 2015

The Lesser Blessed

"For the lesser blessed
it's all promises…
And you'll turn
but, lady, you'll burn…"

—"CELEBRATE" BY FIELDS OF THE NEPHILIM

"He accepted them as a holocaust."

—OLD TESTAMENT, THE BOOK OF WISDOM (3:1–9)

Me

I REMEMBER. IT is the summer of my crucifixion. I try so hard to be pure; I take two baths a day. At least underwater, I can hear my heart beat. The skin on my back dries. Cracks. I make the noise of splitting wood when I walk and my scent is of something crumbling.

I scratch with a knife the word NO a hundred million times on the back of all the mirrors in our house, so my mother sees that I say NO to her, so my mother sees that I say NO to my father, so my mother sees that I say NO to the world, and to the acts unforgivable.

I walk out to the road that leads to Edzo and Yellowknife. I stand daringly close. I wave to the truckers who blare their horns. I am still a child and comfortable waving to strangers.

I see a therapist who asks me to draw how I see myself. I hand in a picture of a forest.

He looks closely, says there is no one. I say, "Look, there. I am already buried."

There is NO a hundred million times on every rock, tree and leaf...

Them

"Firefighters Find Rae Man in Burning House, Fort Rae, N.W.T."
—*The Northern Perspective*

"A DOGRIB MAN died in a smoky blaze Wednesday after fire engulfed his home. Firefighters retrieved the victim's body after the building had burned to the ground. The man died of smoke inhalation and contusions to his skull. Firefighters speculate he fell down while trying to flee the inferno at approximately 10:30 p.m. He was taken to Stanton Yellowknife Hospital by ambulance, where he was pronounced dead on arrival. RCMP and fire department investigators are still trying to determine the cause of the blaze. The victim's name has been withheld until the next of kin have been notified."

Johnny

I'LL NEVER FORGET the first time I saw Johnny Beck. It was in the high school foyer, the first day of school. He was Metis, a half-breed. He wore blue jeans, a jean jacket and white high tops. His hair was feathered and long, his eyes piercing and blue. He had on a black AC/DC shirt. It was the "Who Made Who" one, where this guy is being operated on by aliens. This probably sounds like any typical teen-ager but the thing I remember about Johnny was the look on his face. He looked like he didn't give a white lab rat's ass about anything or anybody. He sat in the foyer next to Darcy McMannus. Darcy was cracking jokes but Johnny wasn't laughing. Johnny had this guarded look about him, like he was carrying the weight of Hell. All the girls were saying, "What's his name? Find out his name!"

I didn't do a thing. I was too busy looking for Juliet Hope. I was also trying to keep a lookout for Jazz the Jackal.

I'm Indian and I gotta watch it.

Mom

"LARRY, JED'S GOING to be coming in soon," my mom said from the living room. She had her glasses on so I knew she was studying. "Something happened to him this summer. He sounded kind of shaken up when he called."

"Is he okay?"

(Don't look at me)

"I hope so," she said.

Jed was the best. He was my mom's boyfriend in a weird sort of way. He'd come into town for a few months and he'd get us all settled as a "family," then he'd leave because of arguments— he'd say it was because he had a job, but I knew the truth. My mom wouldn't marry him. He loved her, he really did, but she was still scared, I guess, of men. Jed was a firefighter, a bush cook, a Ranger, a tour guide and a whole lot of other things as well. He'd been around the world and he always had a story to tell. He was Slavey and proud of it. I wanted him and my mom to get together. I really needed some stability. I know that sounds lame, but it's true.

"When will he get here?" I inquired.

(And listen to my black teeth scream)

"As soon as he can. Hunting season's just beginning."

"Hmph," I mumbled. "I hope he stays for a while."

"He's coming in to inspect the water bombers for the next fire season," she said.

I could see my mom was pretty excited about Jed, so I left her alone. She was cranking CCR and Patsy Cline. That was a good sign. Mostly she just studied, studied, studied. She wanted to be a teacher. She took day and night courses at Arctic College. We had been in Fort Simmer since my accident. It was okay, not much to do if you're not into booze or sports. I mostly read and listened for stories.

I have this lousy memory because of my accident, but if you were to tell me a neat story, I'd be able to tell it back to you years from now, word for word. For example, the last time Jed was here, he told us about a trip to India. I'll tell it to you. It goes like this:

The Blue Monkeys of Corruption

"WELL, I WAS in India one time, eh...

"It was just a regular day and, um, I was smoking up. We were having tea and toast and a pipe. I was passing it around with my buddies and, like, in India every animal is sacred but at the same time there are monkeys in the city that steal. The monkeys were crippled. For punishment, somebody hacked off the hands or arms from the monkey bodies because the monkeys were thieves; they were elegant yet clumsy thieves.

"The monkeys have their own tribes in the city, and I guess the monkeys had been studying me and my buddies. They knew we were stoned happy cripples and monkeys smile like God smiles when the crippled are happy and even more so do the monkeys smile when the crippled are paralyzed. At the time, we were pretty stoned and kept passing the pipe.

"I mean, the tea and the toast were great but the pipe was even better. We were sitting there and we weren't talking because we didn't need to talk. We had reached a new state in our friendship where our speaking was half murdered by the time we got to wrapping our mouths around our words. And these eight monkeys just hopped up on this balcony. They surrounded us.

"I remember thinking if ever I wanted a postcard, I wanted a postcard right then and there. I would have bought a box of twelve pictures of these eight monkeys on this balcony surrounding us as we passed the pipe. They watched us. I think five of them were missing an arm or a hand, and they had these mean eyes. That was the only thing that gave this postcard away. Those eyes. It seemed as if some of these monkeys had killed before in an elevator and the elevator had never been blessed, you know, and the people in India would ride in this elevator all day and they would think: 'Why does this elevator feel so spooky? Is it haunted? Why does it stink?'

"But the monkeys, what they did was they attacked us. They swarmed around us, and this wasn't an unchoreographed attack; this was a very well-thought-out, well-planned manoeuvre. It was timed and it was a postcard nightmare. The eight wonderful monkeys turned into the Blue Monkeys. They scared us and they screamed in these rasps with these carnivorous teeth, these fibula-crunching teeth. I was paralyzed but I realized that if I didn't get out of there, like immediately, these monkeys were in fact going to bite me, and I didn't want shots in India because you don't know what they do to those needles—they could be free-basing Javex with those needles! I don't know! So I ran, because I feared the doctors more than I feared the bite of the Blue Monkeys. We ran into this storm cellar and we locked ourselves in this basement. Those monkeys were hammering on the door even though some of them didn't have hands! They still found ways to hammer this door so it sounded like a million drums on the streets of India. It was awful. It was scary. I screamed like I had never screamed since I was seven. I feared for my life! And we waited and we waited for an hour, a good clean hour, for the Blue Monkeys to go about their business and get whatever they wanted. We just hoped they'd leave us alone because we were tourists in India, for chrissakes. The Blue Monkeys had no right to turn this postcard into something angry or greedy, so I prayed like mad. I meant every inch of that prayer and, if remember correctly, there were tears flowing down my face.

"So the circle was complete, because not only had I screamed but I had prayed. And that's fine, that was release for me, and I guess I needed that at that particular point in my life. An hour later we walked out very carefully to our picnic of tea and toast and the pipe. Everything was gone: our clothes on the hangers were gone; the toast was gone; the butter was gone; the pipe was gone. And, like, I don't know what the monkeys wanted with our pipe but they took it. Perhaps that was the greatest tragedy of all, because we had some great, great hash in that pipe and I was quite upset about the whole thing. I realized at that moment that I had to get out of India.

"If the Blue Monkeys had followed me that far—especially if they could get that far missing hands and arms, I realized I had to go to Africa, the dark continent. I had a feeling the Blue Monkeys would not follow me there."

That's the story he told me. It's yours now. Tell anyone you want.

Mom

MY MOM SAT at her work table watching me. I was in the kitchen. The house was looking good. We had been here for two years and there was a new secondhand shelf for her books. She picked up her coffee and eyed me over her cup.

"Are you going to make banana bread, or what?" I asked.

My mother shrugged, so I carried on. "Well, it's been ages since we've had some."

"Why don't you make bannock? Jed showed you how, didn't he?"

"Do we have raisins?"

She shrugged again, so I got up and started to make bannock. I got my ingredients—flour, sugar, salt, baking powder, lard, water (it has to be luke-warm, that's what Jed taught me) and raisins. My mom went back to typing. While I was sifting the dry ingredients and heating up the lard, I looked at my mom. She'd cut her hair the last time Jed split and it hadn't grown back to its original length. My dad would've called her a dizzy shit for doing that, but I could see why.

Jed told me that if a Dogrib woman cuts her hair she has to burn it. If not, when she dies, she has to go back all through her life and pick up every single hair she ever dropped before going up to heaven. My mom's hair was usually black, but in summer it turned kind of red. She had dark brown eyes that turned black when she got mad. When her and Jed argued, my mom's eyes got so they could incinerate you if you said the wrong thing. These days they were a hazel brown, like the pelt of a cinnamon bear. She was short, about five foot two. I heard Jed once say that out of all the tribes in the Northwest Territories, the Dogrib had the sweetest feet and the softest hands. I'm not psycho or anything, but I had to admit my mom had nice feet.

"You know," she said, "in the olden days, the Dogrib used to put fish eggs in their bannock."

"Oh yummmm," I mimicked and rolled my eyes. "Oh wow." I started rubbing my belly in mock pleasure (watching you) and moaning all around the kitchen. My mom ignored me.

"I'll pass," I sang and plopped an egg in the water.

My mom went back to typing, so I left her alone. After kneading the dough and greasing the baking pan, I placed the bannock in the oven and put the timer on for thirty minutes. Then I blasted some Iron Maiden in my room, and after that some Judas Priest, some Slayer, some Ozzy and more Maiden.

Every song for me was a beautiful forest to get lost in, and every forest reminded me of both Juliet and Jed.

Mister Harris

SCHOOL HAD TAKEN off. We were three weeks into September. I had settled into my classes and was used to the stench of lockers and to my new teachers. Mister Harris had come from Hay River. He and Johnny locked horns right away. On the first day, Mister

Harris, during roll call, looked at Johnny and said, "Mister Beck, you look familiar. Do I know you?"

Johnny retorted, "Yeah, Mister Harris, I'm the guy who passed out on your lawn." Mister Harris glared at him while we all laughed.

Mister Harris was a sad excuse of a man. He had a shark's smile right below his round little nose. His pot belly and bubble butt made him look sadly ballerina-ish as he arched his form to and fro around the classroom. While we read, he would sit quietly stroking his balding head, patting it like a baby's ass or rolling his fingers across it as if it were a delicate pie crust about to crumble. His absent-minded caresses only drew attention to his protruding forehead. He also had that disease where your head shimmy, shimmy, shimmies.

The sad thing about our school was that we were so far behind the system. It's true, and as a result, the students in our school were baby birds falling to their deaths while the school was guilty of failure to breathe. The teachers often sent their own kids down south to get an education. I don't want to mention any names, but Mister Harris was a classic example. He was a blown-human tire. There was this cool thing about him: his index finger. I watched it. It was actually a magic wand that cast the spell of human blush around the room. Whoever he'd point to, they'd blush. He'd point to me, I'd blush.

One day we were having this huge debate about whether it was environment or upbringing that creates a criminal. I looked around. Wasn't it fucking obvious? With the quiet bleeding labour of shellfish in our lockers. The sweet rotting flesh of our feet. The fluorescent lights making me weakdizzydemented. The crab cream two desks over. The gum under my desk. The spits on the floor. The silverfish. The crunch under my runners. The bleeding badge of the sun. The crunch under my runners. My father's teeth. The crunch under my runners. Kevin Garner was selling drugs in the back row. Clarence Jarome was jamming his HB pencil into the primer of a 12-gauge slug. Everybody in the room, as their bodies cooled out, had their eyes fusing shut, and Juliet was nowhere to be found. Johnny Beck had been sighing out loud and roaring his yawns all throughout the class readings. Mister Harris sighed too, and asked Johnny several times to be quiet. Finally, after Johnny had done everything but start bawling out of boredom, Mister Harris stood up and yelled, "Mister Beck. Is there any way that we, as a class, can accommodate you in making this a more enjoyable learning experience?"

Johnny sat up and looked around. He thought about it for a minute; he put his hand to his chin and rubbed an invisible beard. He cocked one brow and everybody giggled.

"As a matter of fact, Mister Harris, yes! Yes, there is something that you, as a teacher of our English class, can do to make this a more enjoyable learning experience."

"I see," Mister Harris said as he paced in front of the room. His magic wand finger flicked erect as he approached the subject. "Mister Beck," he gritted, "oh, please, Mister Beck, enlighten us—what might that be?"

"Well," Johnny said as he stood up, "you have this entire classroom set up wrong."

"What?" Mister Harris spat.

"Yeah, you do. We're all facing that snot-green blackboard. You get to face the windows and the sunlight. Now, wouldn't it be more comfortable if we turned this whole classroom around so we face the sun? Come on. You could feel the last of the summer sun on your back during the day, we'd get to see some sunshine, and everybody's happy. Even you, Mister Harris. What do you think, class?"

Everybody clapped and hooted their appreciation. Johnny sat

down and waited for a reply. There was a thick pause. Mister Harris stood still. We watched him, and he got fatal on us. His little shark face was red. He walked over to the door, opened it and pointed out.

"Get," he ordered.

"What?" everybody said in disbelief. "Come on, Mister Harris. What's the scoop? We'll all help. It'll only take a few minutes. Come on."

When Johnny didn't move, Mister Harris said, "Mister Beck, are we going to start our war all over again?"

"Is that a question?" Johnny asked, picking his teeth.

"That's a question," Mister Harris shimmied. "You and I have discussed your behaviour. We both agreed you would attempt to be a better student."

"I know," Johnny said. "But couldn't we just move things around? Couldn't we just talk?"

"No!" Mister Harris yelled. He scared us and I guess he scared himself too. He sat down and thought about it. The class sat straight. It felt like everyone was screaming inside but couldn't let it out.

"Okay, John," he said. "Let's talk about students who have talent but never even try to reach their potential."

Johnny's voice came from low in his throat when he said, "Okay, Mister Harris. Let's talk about a teacher whose wife is leaving him."

The air in the classroom dropped. Mister Harris stood and paced. "Let's talk about boys who have no father and a mother who's—"

Johnny stood up and shouted, "No! Let's talk about a teacher who drinks too much!"

Mister Harris yelled, "Getthehellouttahere!" and pointed to the door. Johnny walked out with his head down, and just as he neared the door, he spun around and pointed. "You're a tough man, babyfingers," he said, and we all started laughing. I couldn't believe it.

"Get out!!" Mister Harris roared.

Johnny left, and the class was quiet for five solid minutes.

"I believe," Mister Harris said, stammering to resurrect the class, "that it is every parent's nightmare to watch his child become a social misfit."

"I believe," I said inside, "it is every parent's dream to watch his child burn."

Six Stages of Rigor Mortis

LATER THAT MORNING we had a class with Mademoiselle Sauvé. French. My desk was in the middle of the room. Johnny's seat was empty. He usually sat right next to me. Darcy McMannus was hunched over his desk in the far back corner. I knew Juliet had a spare in the library.

Sometimes I'd go to the bathroom and pass by there real slow. (Juliet! Juliet! Juliet!)

I don't know why we took French. Personally, I hated it. The guidance counsellor said we'd get into college and university a lot easier. For crisis management, I only went because of Mademoiselle Sauvé's French titties. They were so perky. I swear to God I'm perverted or something, but I just can't help noticing. I can't help it. I have hungers, you know. Man hungers…

We were going through the six stages of rigor mortis, droning on and on about the verb être, which means "to be." It didn't mean a damn thing to me, but I had it down pat: "Je suis, tu es, il est, elle est, nous sommes, vous êtes, ils sont, elles sont." I was with the rest of the damn worker bees singing this death chant mantra when we heard a great rumbling. It sounded like somebody was dragging heavy pieces of wood across the floor. The floor vibrated under our feet. Nobody could figure it out. Dean Meddows mentioned maybe they were setting up for a student assembly but Moustache Sammy said no, that couldn't be right. The rumbling was on this floor, next door. English class! Mister Harris's room! Somebody was moving the classroom furniture—Johnny!

We all sat up. The girls giggled and whispered things to each other. The boys smiled and looked out the windows, but Mademoiselle Sauvé kept on with her class nonetheless.

"Johnny Beck," Junior Merc said, "now that's a man with balls."

"Bullshit," Darcy McMannus countered from the corner. "He's a goddamn pain in the ass, that's what he is."

We were all quiet after that, 'cause Darcy was the boss. I snuck a peek over at Johnny's empty desk, and I noticed that scratched into the wood-top was "Johnny Beck was here questing for fire" and "Stay high pigs don't fly" and "I don't go to high school, I go to school high" and "Juliet Hope goes down."

As the rumbling in the next room continued, a religious fervour swept over the room. A human cry arose from student lips. We bombarded Mademoiselle Sauvé with a roar of "JE SUIS! TU ES! IL EST! ELLE EST! NOUS SOMMES! VOUS ÊTES! ILS SONT! ELLES SONT!"

I looked out of the corner of my eye and even Darcy McMannus was cheering...a little.

We all ran out of the classroom when the buzzer went off and peeked into the next room. Johnny wasn't there but his signature was: the whole classroom had been rearranged. Mister Harris's desk had its back to the windows so he could feel the heat of September's dying light. The class could look forward to watching the November sunsets at four in the afternoon. If anyone had to serve a detention or work late, they could watch the Christmas moon come out at 3:30. The picture of the Queen with her big hooters was placed to the left of the bookshelf; the plastic glory of Mister Harris's plants was by his desk. Even the clock that timed our sagging hours was there, above the window right behind Mister Harris's desk. I laughed and the class laughed with me. We had our hero.

The next day, however, the classroom furniture was moved back to its original position. Mister Harris kept diligently to his curriculum while we looked at the snot-green chalkboard. We didn't see Johnny for a whole week. He had been suspended.

The Feast of Kings

JOHNNY CAME BACK on Monday. I watched him all day. After class, I ran up behind him as he walked across the field leading towards the back streets of town where we lived.

"Boy, that Mister Harris," I said. "What a Leonard."

"Leonard who?"

"Not a who—a what."

"Who-Babyfingers?"

"Yeah."

"The fuck's a Leonard?" he asked. I could tell he was interested.

"Oh, you know, a monge, a face-melt, a stick!"

"What?"

"An asshole!" I yelled. We both smiled after that. "My name's Larry Sole."

"Johnny Beck."

"Man, you sure are daring."

"You're only beautiful once."

"How's it going?"

"Don't ask."

"Okay. Wanna see where I live? I'm on Little Vietnam—"

"Little Vietnam?"

"It's just around the corner from you. My mom goes to the college. Is your mom a college student? My mom's a college student."

I remembered Mister Harris saying something about Johnny's mom but I didn't want to pry.

"Yeah, howdjoo guess?"

"Spruce Manor's the town residence for college students."

"My mom's going there," he mumbled. "This town sucks. I mean, if this town were a fart, I wouldn't even stop to sniff it. I'd just keep on walking."

I laughed and covered my mouth.

"This high school any good?"

"The chicks here have magnormous breasts."

He looked at me. "It's the pill, man. You gotta love it."

I inhaled autumn. It was blazing along our path. The fireweed surrounding us sang with her brightest voice: purple, bloody, fresh. I almost didn't see the empty Lysol bottles or the brown broken glass we walked by.

"My number's in the book," I said. "If you want to go for a pop, give me a call—holy shit!"

"What?" Johnny asked, but I was already running to the house.

"Ravens!" I yelled. "The damn ravens!"

It was too late. The ravens had opened the garbage bin and scattered our garbage over the lawn and road. It was five minutes of death. There were juice cans, coffee filters, caribou bones, everything, just everything you'd never want to see on your goddamn lawn.

"What the hell happened?" Johnny asked as he jogged up to me.

"Those damn ravens got into the garbage again. I was supposed to put another lock on the door. The ravens keep picking the old one."

"Ravens can't do that—"

"Damn straight," I said. "I've seen ravens steal food from a baby's hand. They're real bastards when it comes right down to it."

"Wow."

"Well, could you help me?" I asked.

"I think," he said, "I'm gonna be a Leonard and get the hell home. My mom'll be home at five."

"Suit yourself."

"Yeah. You can come over later if you want. Bring food—or call me. Ask for the Big Kahoona."

"You bet!" I called out. "I'll do that. Sol later." "Sol later" is Raven Talk. It's "See you later" said really fast. The correct response is "Sol" but Johnny didn't say it. All he did was shake his head and go, "Little Vietnam. Not bad, not bad."

I went into the house to grab more garbage bags.

Bannock and Dishes

THE STICKER BY the apartment 13 slot said "A. Beck," and seeing how Johnny's last name was Beck, I rang it. I had some hot bannock wrapped in a plastic bag stuffed in my jacket. The intercom crackled and I called out, "Johnny, this is Larry, I'm—"

"Hello?" Johnny asked. "Hello, am I on the air? Can I make a request? Just wait, someone else wants to make a request…oh, piss on it—this thing is broken. Just come up." The buzzer went off and I opened the door.

Spruce Manor, I thought, what a place to die. There was the smell of wet rugs, muktuk and dry meat in the air. I breathed through my mouth and covered my nose. People had punched holes in the wall all the way up the stairs. Johnny was standing out in the hallway with the door open. From his apartment I could hear AC/DC. It was either "Back in Black" or "Highway to Hell." I didn't really know them. AC/DC was great to dance to but I never bought any of their tapes. Johnny had his shirt sleeves rolled up to his elbows; his hair was kind of messy. He had on bleached white socks with a hole in one of them. As I got closer, I noticed he had soap suds on his hands.

"*Edanat'e*?" I said.

"Which?"

"That means, How are you?"

"Oh…good. Come on in. I'm just cleaning up the joint. It's Larry, right?"

"Yup," I said, "and you're the Big Kahoona."

"Yeah." He looked nervous.

I walked into the apartment and took off my jacket. I carefully hung it up, away from the dirty floor.

"What's this?" Johnny asked as I handed him the hot package.

"Don't panic," I answered. "I made bannock."

"Oh yeah?" Johnny smiled. "That's cool, man. That's really cool. Come in."

We walked through the kitchen. Johnny had done a motherload of dishes. They were stacked right up and there were still more to do. Ashtrays on the kitchen table were overflowing. There were about three different sets of cards, all of which looked overused. There was a crib board there too, but I didn't know how to play. I sat on the love seat in the living room and Johnny turned down the volume. The apartment was barren. I mean, there was nothing on the walls except for a Canadian flag that reached from one end of the room to the other, covering the windows completely. There was a TV, but it was piled on some old milk crates. I noticed the linoleum was peppered with burns where people had dropped their cigarettes and matches. The holes looked like charred, blurred eyes staring up at the ceiling.

I remembered the flag from school had been stolen recently and eyed this one more carefully.

"You like country?" he asked.

"Sure."

"Hey, is it true there's a song called 'Take Your Tongue Outta My Mouth, I'm Trying to Kiss You Good-bye?'"

"What!"

"Jokes! You like AC/DC?"

I wrinkled my nose. "Iron Maiden rules."

"Oh yeah, 'Run to the Hills,' hey? Did you butter this already?"

"Yeah. Do you have any raspberry jam?"

"Naw, we're strapped until my mom gets some cash. Things are pretty horror-show right now."

"What?" I said, eyeing him. "Ain't nothing sadder than bannock without raspberry jam—that's just about as sad as a one-bark dog!" (Jed taught me that one.) "Well, how about lard? You got any lard?"

"Nope."

"You know what they say? Bannock and lard make you hard!"

"Cute," he smirked.

From the hallway, a little boy peeked around the corner. He had big eyes, like a whitefish. He walked past Johnny and sat at the table across from me.

"Edanat'e?" I asked.

"The hell does that mean?" the little guy asked.

"How are you, smart ass, and be nice to Larry. He's in my class," Johnny snapped. "Look what he brought us."

"Is that bannock?"

"Yeah, and you owe another twenty-five cents to the swear-jar."

"What!?" the little guy said. "What for, huh? What did I say?"

"You said, 'What the hell does that mean?' 'Hell' is on the list. You owe twenty-five cents."

"Damn," the little guy agreed. "Can I pay later when Mom gives me allowance?"

"No," Johnny said."You pay it now, and that's another twenty-five cents, Mister Damn."

Frowning, the boy pulled two quarters out of his pocket and put them into a glass jar in the middle of the supper table. The jar was half full. The quarters clinked as they landed on the top of the pile.

"Good boy," Johnny said. "Now don't swear."

I looked at Johnny and motioned to the jar.

"Scoop?" I asked.

"Scoop…where?"

"No, what's the scoop? With the jar?"

"Oh that." He smiled. "If Donny swears he puts twenty-five cents into the swear-jar. If he calls anyone a name, that's another twenty-five cents in the jar. If he talks back or starts to hit, that's another quarter. I use the money to do the laundry and buy milk or juice."

"Ever smart," I said.

"It's 'cause of my big cock, I guess!" Johnny joked.

"Ischa!" I said and laughed.

They both studied me.

"You some kind of chief or what?" Donny asked.

Before I could answer, he asked, "How much money you got, chief?"

"Two bucks."

"Well," he said, eyeing my pockets, "if I can guess where you were born, I can keep it, 'kay?"

"What are you going to do with the cash if you win?"

"He's saving up for a mountain bike," Johnny muttered. "He's already got a hundred dollars so far."

"Okay," I said. There was no damn way he could know I was born in Fort Rae. "Where was I born?"

He eyeballed me and grinned. "You were born between your mama's legs!"

We all started laughing.

"He's a bandit," Johnny smiled, looking at Donny.

"Hand it over," Donny commanded. I gave him his cash.

"Thanks, chief," he said as he stuffed the bills into his shirt pocket. "You got hair on your nuts, or what?"

Before I could answer, Johnny stomped over to Donny, scooped him up and took him around the corner. The little boy was quiet about the whole thing, and it looked like this had been done many times before. They were gone for about thirty seconds. Only Johnny came back.

"Sorry, Lare," he said. "My brother can be a putz."

I didn't say anything. Johnny took a break from doing the dishes and had some bannock. I was thinking of having some too, but the way he was taking great big mouthfuls, it looked like he hadn't eaten in a long time.

"Hey, this is goob," he said.

"Not too dry?" I asked.

"Naw, just right. Goob." Johnny seemed to be antsy about me being there. He kept mentioning that his mom would be home soon and that she liked it really quiet.

"Nothing personal, Lare, but you better go before she gets here. Thanks for the bannock. I still have to do those dishes."

"Yeah. Tell Donny I said good-bye."

"You gotter." He nodded. He looked at the clock, then walked me to the hall. I wasn't even out the door yet and he was already back in the kitchen scrubbing away.

The next time I saw Johnny was in the hallway at school. Except it wasn't him that I saw first—it was the fight he was in and the commotion it caused.

There were students all around him, buzzing like bees excited or about to swarm. There were about thirty guys—Chipewyan, Cree, Slavey, Inuit and white—with their arms locked to form a huge human circle so nobody in the ring could escape until it was all over. If whoever was fighting tried to escape, they'd be kicked back into the ring. People who were late were pushing into the circle to watch the fight. The air was charged and people were yelling out things like: "Kick his honky ass!" "Don't be a pussy… fight!! fight!" "Fiiiiidemm !"

Johnny had his fists raised, and his face was ruby red. The way his fists were guarding his face, I could tell he was no stranger to scraps. It wasn't until I pushed into the crowd that I saw who he was scrapping. Johnny Beck was fighting Darcy McMannus!

Darcy

I HAVE TO tell you about Darcy McMannus. He was the whitest, meanest, toughest, rowdiest and most feared bully in town. It was rumoured that he had a police record and that he used to fight his uncles for money. He was slow but powerful. Jed once told me a story about an old grizzly charging a moose. That old grizzly was Darcy, and he stood now with the stance of a boxer. Darcy had fat fingers and scarred knuckles. His thick forearms rippled when he gripped a bat or whaled on somebody's skull. He was shy when he was sober but vicious when drunk. I knew Darcy as a slow dinosaur who had a chunky ass, which, in all honesty, was getting chunkier. He used to play hockey until his knees blew, and often in the locker room I would study the metal knee braces embedded in his meaty shins. Darcy always wore a leather hockey jacket that said "Timber Wolves" on the back in faded orange letters and "Center" over the right bicep. The jacket was thick and faded, and Darcy never zipped it up. When he would smoke across the street, off school property, I could see steam rising from his chest as his body heat met the autumn chill.

Darcy walked with a limp. Sometimes it was his left knee and sometimes it was his right leg that gave him problems. He always wore grey track pants and never any ginch. His horse cock would jiggle through the cotton as he limped down the main hallway. I once saw two grade eight babes walk past him with wide, bulging eyes and whisper in glee as his tired, dark shadow slowly passed over them.

"Oh my God," one swooned, "it's ever big!"

"Ever!" the other agreed.

"Oh, Darcy," I prayed as I studied him now, "get your skull crushed, get that moose cock of yours kicked. Bleed for a day, Darcy, bleed for a day."

And, as if in agreement with my plea, a fist blurred its way into Darcy's fat face so quickly it snapped back before Darcy could make a sound. The sound was shock. Darcy made an "oh" in recoil, and then began his bleeding. I'm not talking trickle-trickle. I'm talking a faucet of blood gushing down his shirt, his grey gym pants and all over his fat runners. Darcy's eyes were watering, and I could tell he wanted out of the fight pretty bad. He kept his guard up, close to his spurting face.

"Hey, b...backstabber," Darcy hissed around his hands, "y... you think you're so tough 'cause you sucker-punched me? Next time I see you, you're going down."

"Thumper, you fat fuck. You can't touch me," Johnny said and smiled. I stood there awestruck. I think we all were. Darcy put his splashed hands down when he saw the principal and three other teachers come running towards the circle. The teachers tried to push through but the students had their arms locked tight. It was a good thirty-second struggle. Then Mister Harris showed up.

"Break it up. Break it up," he called out, and pushed through the crowd. "What in hell's name is going on here?"

When he saw Johnny Beck with his fists up and the blood faucet down Darcy's body, he decided who the culprit was.

"Beck!" he yelled, "get your ass to my office!"

With that, he grabbed Johnny and pushed him in the general direction of the office. But Johnny reeled around and caught Mister Harris's grip and sent him off balance. Mister Harris staggered back about two feet into the crowd. I swear to God the whole school fell silent, even Darcy. It was like everyone was holding their breath. If there's one thing you do not do, you never touch a teacher. Johnny took that moment, turned around and walked right out of the school.

"Screw you, Harris!" somebody yelled around the corner. "We were just trying to keep the circle strong!"

Everybody laughed but me. It was Jazz the Jackal.

"Back to your classes," Harris ordered. "Anyone out in the hallway gets a week's detention."

The next thing I knew everyone had dispersed and gone quickly to their next class. All I remember was glancing to my right and seeing the look on Mister Harris's face. His little head shimmied back and forth as if he were agreeing with someone or deciding on something.

I, like the rest of the school, got the hell out of there and went straight to Math.

It was two days later when Johnny called. "Hello?"

"Larry. Johnny Beck here. Just calling to remind you what a stud I am. Listen...let's go for coffee."

"Sure, man. Hey, you kicked Darcy's ass the other day. What was the fight all about anyways?"

"Not now. Someday I'll tell you about me and Thumper— maybe when you're older."

"Where do you want to meet?"

"Pinebough."

"Half an hour?"

"Nope, fifteen."

"Kay."

"Later."

"Mkbuh." That's Raven talk for "Okay bye." We say it really fast and that's how it comes out.

Our Beginning

THE PINEBOUGH WAS the teen-age hangout in Fort Simmer. The first thing you noticed when you walked in was the smoke. The room was blue with it. I swear to God if I have an iron lung ten years from now it will be because I used to hang around that place. It was the kind of smoke that stuck to your clothes and skin. It made your hair all tough and scratchy, and your nostrils burned if you hung there too long.

Definitely not a place to do it doggy-style!

I walked in and Johnny was waiting for me. His back was to the wall and he had a coffee in his hand. He smiled as I walked towards him. On the other side of the cafe were all the other downtown regulars. They watched Johnny and sniffed the air like wolves. The Shandells were droning, "Crimson and clover, over and over."

Johnny was about my height, but I had spaghetti arms and daddy-longlegs. My clothes just hung on me. I wasn't a threat to anyone and, in turn, people just looked past me when they were looking for a fight. Believe me, this was a blessing. I pulled a chair out and sat on it like a tough guy, sticking my ass out and plopping down really hard.

"How's she going?" he asked.

"Not bad. How come you decided to call?"

Johnny's hair was picture perfect and he wore a muscle T-shirt even though it was almost October and only two above. He took a sip of his coffee and smiled. "Well, Lare, if you must know, the Big Kahoona has the strangest urge to hump the skinniest boy in town!"

"Oh, man," I laughed, "you're rude."

"Yeah," he agreed. "I'm a Leonard."

"How's Donny?"

"Donny's Donny," he said. "Guy's already reading porno mags. I found his stash yesterday. Man, I wanted that guy to be a kid just a little bit longer."

"Hmmm," I said, trying to think of a way to change the subject. "Did you know that if you lie really still at night and listen to your tummy—if you just listen, you can hear all sorts of machinery?"

"Yeah?"

"Yeah, and if you lie there long enough your asshole will start to itch."

"Really?"

"Really, and if your asshole starts to itch, that's your tapeworm peeking out!"

"Ha ha!" he laughed. "You're bent."

"Hey," I said. "Don't laugh at my tapeworm. At night he comes out and we play."

That broke the ice. We must have talked all afternoon. He told me about Hay River, the place he just came from. He went on and on about what a party town it was, and I asked why he had left.

He winked. "There was no one left to fuck."

He went on again about how he hated Simmer and how he couldn't wait to live with his dad when things settled down with his parents' divorce. His dad was trying to get a job in Yellow-knife, and if he got it, he was gonna come get his boys before moving on. I had a coffee and we shared a plate of fries. After the conversation that afternoon, we were inseparable.

"Take your tongue out of my mouth," he said. "I'm trying to kiss you good-bye."

The ketchup bottle farted onto the plate.

Moose and Mom

"WHEN ARE YOU going to get us a moose?" my mom asked. She had already downed half a pot of coffee.

"Take it easy. I just got up."

"When Jed gets here I want you two to go hunting."

"What? The last time we went hunting I almost got shot in the ass!"

"Larry, he didn't know he had dropped shells by the fire. They were in his shirt pocket and fell out. Give him a break."

"So he says!"

"Larry, I'm serious. Get us a moose or some caribou."

"We'll see," I said. "We'll see."

Hazing

DON'T ASK ME why, but every high school across the land has had at one time or another an initiation process. Some schools call it Hazing. I call it Hell. At our school, all new students and teachers had to go on stage and be auctioned off like slaves. The money was raised for the graduating class and paid for the dance and booze. A lot of yard work got done throughout the town and a lot of cars got cleaned, but any survivor of the ordeal would tell you a lot of grievances got settled that week and a lot of kids got hurt. Johnny Beck, newcomer to town, was the hottest commodity to come to Fort Simmer in a long time.

I had already gone through my slave day when I entered the

school in grade eight. Garth Chaplin bought me. I had to paint the ten-inch cock on the eight-foot plastic horse on top of Harv's Resort a lovely lullaby red. What was I thinking? Trauma, that's what.

The slave auction was held about a month after school got settled. By that time, people had already made up their minds who they wanted. I think half the school wanted Johnny. The other half wanted Sean McMannus, Darcy's younger brother. Because they couldn't beat up Darcy and they suffered under his rule, his younger brother was a heat-score. And you can bet that whoever got him would make him suffer.

I got there after the auction was already rolling. The gymnasium was alive with yelling and laughter. People were throwing their hands in the air trying to attract the eyes of the judges while the silent lambs waited up on stage to be led off. I sat back and watched people buy and claim souls. I saw people get ugly when they were outbid and I saw the guppy eyes of the lambs widen when they saw who they had been sold to. I kept thinking what a tragic waste of energy and love it was. After all, I could have been doing it doggy-style!

It was about an hour before they brought out Johnny. It was no mistake he was the last to be sold. His hands were tied and his shirt was off for the slavelike effect. People roared and cheered when he was led out onto the stage. The lights were turned down throughout the gymnasium and the spotlight focussed on him. He glared at the audience.

"All right, buyers and sellers of souls," called the auctioneer, "we have before us the young man who's raised a lot of eyebrows lately, coming from Hay River and attending grade eleven. Let's give Johnny Beck a warm welcome."

The floor and walls shook. People were stomping their feet and whistling all around me.

The auctioneer smiled and said, "Let's start the bidding."

The lights were turned on and people fell silent. They were reaching into their pockets and striking bets.

"Do I hear ten dollars?" the auctioneer called.

"Twelve dollars!" somebody shouted.

"Oooooooooooo," the crowd responded, and we all laughed.

"Do I hear fifteen?"

"Twenty!" someone hollered. The bidding had begun.

People who were broke or satisfied with their purchases left for deeds that needed to be done. There were quite a few of us left, though, mostly people with their arms crossed eyeing the buyers.

The price rose and rose. People stomped off mad and sweaty when the pot got too high, and soon it was at a hundred and ten dollars.

"Do I hear a hundred and fifteen?"

We all looked around. A hundred and fifteen? This was a record.

"A hundred and fifteen!" somebody called from the back of the gym. It was Darcy McMannus. He stood in his old Timber Wolves jacket with his thick moose cock jutting under his track pants. His big ape face had a smile on it that was the meanest I've ever seen.

"A hundred and twenty!" another voice called out. We all craned our necks and stood up to see who it was. It was Mister Harris, standing by the water fountain. His smile wasn't as big as Darcy's but it was just as ugly.

The auctioneer howled, "Do I hear a hundred and thirty?"

"One hundred and forty!"

"One hundred and fifty!"

"One hundred and fifty-five!"

"One hundred and sixty!"

"One hundred and sixty-five!"

Our goose-necks were snapping left and right trying to keep up with the haggling. When it got to one hundred and ninety-five, we all looked at Darcy. He stood alone. I could tell he was broke. His knuckles were white and his jaw tensed. He turned and slammed the gym door behind him.

We looked at Mister Harris. He pulled out his chequebook and ran his hand over his scalp.

"A hundred and ninety-five going once," the auctioneer yelled.

There was a pause. Mister Harris was the last bidder. It looked like he might get Johnny after all.

"Going twice—"

"Two hundred!" a girl's voice called out. This time, we all stood on our chairs to see who it was. We fell silent. It was Juliet Hope.

A Little Info on Juliet Hope Cuz I'm Big Daddy Love

JULIET STOOD OFF to the side of the crowd, right where Darcy had been. She was carrying her black purse and wearing her tight black pants, the ones I liked her in best. She had on a light blue shirt that wasn't tucked in, which was a shame because it meant we couldn't see her ass, and her ass was a marvellous thing. It was not an ass that you could honour with words. If you've ever seen sand dunes in the Sahara, that was her ass. It was not a bubble butt (which is protruding) or a bannock butt (which is flat); instead, it was an ass that sank into the legs after a brief but admirable lift. My hands ached and sang for the chance to grab it!

P.S.

I heard she liked it doggy-style!

But, alas, enough of her ass. It's really her face I want to talk about. Juliet Hope was white and pure. She had the face of an angel, with dark green eyes the colour of grass on a rainy day.

She could suck a man dry with those eyes of hers—and her teeth! They were perfect and straight, and her lips, oh her lips, were thin but erotic. After the nuclear war, when we all turned cannibal and started to eat one another, she would not be involved. Her mouth and teeth would not eat dead things. She would be above all that.

I have never understood women and their noses. Personally, I have a huge nose. It's quite bionic when you see it from the side. But girls have these perfect noses, petite, and Juliet's was no exception. Her skin was perfect, not like mine. No blemishes, no greasy forehead, no cracks or lizard skin. There was only her, Juliet. And I adored her seven dreams deep.

If you've ever heard "High School Confidential" by Rough Trade, it was written for Juliet Hope. She stood about five foot four and her feet were small, like the porcelain-perfect feet of Jesus on the cross. She wore men's shirts that were too big for her, and her dark brown hair was as light as the air that lifted it. She had trimmed it a while ago and kept it loose, to the bottoms of her shoulder blades.

When Juliet was standing off school property, having a smoke, I'd watch her from my English, French and Social Studies classrooms. Every time I went to a dance, I sat where I could see her. When she bent over in her miniskirt to snub out her smoke, I would sit up and moan. When I spied her taking a breath, I breathed deep and held it like a child or a memory. If only she'd show me her breasts, she would make my life's journey so much easier.

In school, Juliet sat like a boy: legs spread, leaning back. In the halls she strutted like an on-duty lifeguard. If she ever decided to put out all the fires she'd started, all the boys would be using crutches. Speaking of which, when I first came here, Juliet was on crutches. I heard a girl saying on the bus that the reason Juliet had to use them was because she had herpes. I never believed it, though. I never did.

A pause from the auctioneer brought me back to the gym. I guess I had faded away and had a series of minor strokes.

"Sold!" he yelled. "It's all over but the crying! My name is Kevin Garner. That concludes this year's Slave Day Auction. Get fucked, get laid, mony mony!"

Holy shit. Everybody laughed and howled. I couldn't believe he had said that. But there were no teachers left. They'd waddled off to the staff room to bloat and stink and die.

Johnny was led off stage to where Juliet stood smiling and happy. As he put on his white T-shirt, I saw Juliet blushing and checking him out. I mean, her eyes touched him all the way up and all the way down. Johnny looked serious as he walked up to her, and she said something to him that made him smile. Somebody said that she paid cash for him and would have paid more.

Because my love for Juliet has claimed me, I must tell you more. She had a reputation for being easy. I heard her called every name in the book. Clarence Jarome once told me in gym class that you could get the dose just by looking at her. Girls talked about her in hushed tones and boys dragged her name out real slow, but to me she was like the first crocus of spring: a gift for everyone.

She was the first girl in grade school to swear at a teacher, break up with a boy and wear make-up. Like 98 per cent of the school population, she was into drugs and alcohol, but it was who she partied with that gave her a reputation. She partied with guys like Darcy "Hose Cock" McMannus and Jazz the Jackal in places across the Alberta border where you could drink without showing ID. Every one agreed they were pretty cool for trekking all the way out there to get hamburgered. (That's Raven talk for "drunk.")

I think in another life I was a great Dogrib hunter who had

Juliet in my sights. She was a white caribou, pure. I believe I let her go out of respect and awe.

Juliet, Jed and the Jesus in Snow

THAT NIGHT I walked down to where Old Man Ferguson kept his dogs, and with my feet I created two incredible hearts in the snow. I'm talking as big as Miami. I had to jump across the outline of the hearts to make letters inside them, and I did a little jig when I was finished. One heart said, "JED + MOM T.L.F.E." with a huge arrow slicing through it. T.L.F.E. equalled "True Love Forever." The other heart, the bigger one, said, "LARRY + JULIET T.I.D." T.I.D. equalled "True If Destroyed."

T.I.D. was a subclause in the contract of love. It meant that any act of God, dog or melting that destroyed the snow I drew the heart on would make it so. With that, I prayed that a squirrel would run across the heart or a spruce bough would fall upon it or an owl would butcher something, anything, in the middle of the heart to break the spell and make it real.

Next Day (flash burns)

JOHNNY HAD THAT "Hello! I just fucked your wife!" smile on his face the next day when he waltzed into the locker room. All the boys surrounded him.

"C'mon, man," Moustache Sammy said, "we saw what happened yesterday. How was she? Is she a scratcher or a screamer?"

"Yeah," Leon pried. "Come on."

Johnny smiled slyly. "Gentlemen, she was pretty decent."

Clarence Jarome watched him. "Nice buds or what?"

Johnny tilted his head back, smiled, and flicked up both thumbs. "Playboy."

"Ya hoo!" we yelled. "All right! Way to go."

Johnny marched around the locker room in full plume glory. His feathered hair was bouncing with him and his blue eyes glittered with glee. He looked at me and winked; I hollered louder than anyone else and followed the king as he strutted out the door.

When I saw Juliet in the hallway by her locker, I stopped. She had so many purple hickeys on her neck it looked as if someone had tried to strangle her. I turned and walked away.

Nice fuckin' deal...

I got a phone call that night. It was Johnny.

"Larry, baby," he purred, "Friday night, you and me are going to a party."

Bash

I DIDN'T KNOW whose house we were going to party at. All I knew was that Juliet had invited Johnny and Johnny had invited me. I was very nervous, but being the Ambassador of Love, I figured this was my chance to be around Juliet.

I wore my newest black jeans and my whitest socks. I ironed my black Iron Maiden "Powerslave" T-shirt, the one where Eddy is on the pyramids in Egypt. I showered and I even flossed my teeth. I met Johnny outside his place. He had showered too, and the part in his hair was perfect. His feathered hair looked like the wing tips of ravens, they whispered so thinly at the ends. He wore faded Levi's and had a thick red cotton shirt. He left the top three buttons undone so you could see his chest hair. He had a little patch that he liked to show off; I guess that was one of the benefits of being Metis. He was wearing a jean jacket, and as he lit a smoke, his hair fell over his face.

"You packin' rubbers?" he asked.

"Naw," I sniffed, "don't need 'em."

"What?" His eyes went big.

"I'm so damn hot, my women buy my rubbers for me—I'm a safe sex sonovabitch!"

"Jesus," he smirked, "I thought you were serious."

"Just joshing. Coulda been, though—I'm something!"

He shook his head, smiling. "Leonard."

"Is your mom home?"

Johnny tensed up. "Yeah, why?"

"Just wonderin' if sometime I could meet her."

"Larry," he answered, "that's one woman you never want to meet."

"Wow," I said. "Shereshly?" That's Raven talk for "Seriously."

"Seriously. Let's go."

Johnny didn't know where the house was, but I did. It was by Conibear Park. It was in the Welfare Centre, a pretty rough part of town. We knocked on the door and were greeted by an older woman. She was dressed up, and I could tell she was off to the Friday night dance. Her hair was still wet and she didn't have any make-up on. I could smell her shampoo and her perfume, the combination of which smelled like rust metal roses. I could see her cleavage: Bananas!

"Hey," this perfect stranger said, looking at me, "you're Verna's boy, ain't ya? I used to live on your street."

"Yes, ma'am," I said, all flushed and hot. I didn't recognize her but was too embarrassed to say anything.

"You men here for Juliet?" she asked.

"Yeah," Johnny said. "She here?"

"Yeah," the woman said, turning around and walking into the house. "She's putting my kids to bed."

Johnny and I stood outside.

"Do we go in?" I asked stupidly.

"I guess," he shrugged. I stopped in the porch and took off my shoes.

"Pussy," Johnny scoffed, "taking off your shoes at a house party. What a putz." He dropped his jacket on the floor on top of a small shelf that held boots. I hissed and hung it up. My mom never allowed anyone in our house to drop a jacket or hat. If you do and a woman steps over your clothes, that's it. You're done for: bad luck and you'll never catch a moose. I hung it up for him and carefully hung mine up too.

Like I said, I'm Dogrib: I gotta watch it.

"Hey, man," I whispered, "I got respect for the lady and her house."

"Yeah, yeah," he said. He pushed me aside and walked into the kitchen.

The woman came out of one of the hallways, towelling her hair. "Juliet'll be out in a few minutes. Hey!" she yelled with wide eyes when she saw Johnny's runners on her kitchen floor. "Whatsa matter with you—ain't you got no respect?"

Johnny turned around and pushed past me. His face was red as he took off his shoes.

"Bitch," he whispered.

"Hey, Juliet," the lady called out. "You picked yourself a real winner."

"Oh, Auntie," Juliet said as she rounded the corner. She had a lit smoke and an ashtray in the same hand. "Relax."

"Hi, Juliet," I called softly. I couldn't look at her. I just looked down at her clothes. She had on those black jeans, the ones that I liked the best. She was also wearing a cool blue shirt. As always, her hair and her make-up were perfect.

"Hi, Larry," she said. "Come in."

I could tell she was disappointed I had come. Now I felt like a Leonard. When she saw Johnny, her eyes lit up and her smile changed: this time it reached her eyes.

Johnny and I sat on the couch. Juliet was talking to her auntie in the kitchen. I read a magazine while Johnny kept messing up my hair.

"You're not going to get any tonight, Larry-poo," he said. "You got monkey-hair."

"Maaaan," I dragged, "don't touch the hair. Besides, it doesn't look like this is a party after all."

"Yeah," Johnny said as he eyed the place, "you're right. I thought this was going to be a shaker. I wonder what they're doing tonight in Hay? Man, they sure know how to party in Hay."

The living room had a huge TV, a cheap stereo and a black velvet Elvis singing to the guests at the Last Supper. There were hippie beads for doors in the house; they hung down like dead spaghetti. The lights were red, which was really neat. Heart was howling, "Let me go crazy crazy on youuuuuuu...."

"Hey, goofs," Juliet's auntie called out, "don't bust my stereo, don't wake up my kids, and leave the food in the fridge alone. There's pop and chips in the pantry."

"Okay." I jumped up. "See you! Have a good time!"

Johnny elbowed me and said, "Kiss-ass."

"Hey, man," I answered, sitting down, "I got respect."

"Ooooooooo," Johnny said, widening his eyes in mock admiration.

We sat there not knowing what to do. I kept trying to pretend I was reading something mighty interesting and Johnny turned on the TV with the remote. He kept flicking through the channels.

"So," Juliet said when she walked into the room. "What do you boys want to do tonight?" She kept looking at Johnny. Johnny stared at the TV.

"Dunno," he said. "Who's all coming over?"

"Oh," she sighed, "whoever wants to, I guess."

I kept my mouth shut. This was my first party and I didn't want to blow it. I noticed that Johnny was playing it cool, not making eye contact. Juliet kept staring at the clock.

When Juliet got tired of trying to pry answers out of Johnny, she began to talk to me. At first I just answered yes or no, but I soon found myself talking to her and loving it.

"Tsa full moon tonight," I said. "Does the full moon make you crazy?"

"No. Something else," she answered and crossed her legs. "What?"

"Lonely," she said, sliding her hands between her thighs and looking at Johnny. "The full moon makes me lonely."

"Humph," I said, looking at the situation. "If I ever swallowed the barrel," I thought, "it would be under a full moon. My mouth would be full of water when I did it. Just like Shamus told me. The pressure of the water would take my head clean off..."

"Hey, want to see some puppies? My auntie's dog just had a litter."

"I got allergies," I explained.

"Are you serious?" she asked. "They've been up here all day. We usually keep them in the basement. Shouldn't you be itching and scratching or something?"

"It's only if I see the puppies, then my eyes get all watery and I get itchy."

"Sounds like you're suppressing something," she said.

"Yeah," Johnny said, "like his little happy hard-on."

"More like my whole fuckin' life," I said.

As they laughed, the doorbell rang.

"Well, look who's here," Darcy said as he walked into the kitchen. He had a bottle of Jack Daniels in his right hand and a case of beer in his left. He had his eyes on Johnny, and the way he was gripping that bottle you could tell he was itching to scrap.

Johnny stood up, his face flushed. His hands were fists and he stood his ground.

I stood up too and walked towards Darcy. Juliet was behind him, saying something I couldn't hear.

Darcy stopped when he saw me. A smile crept across his face.

"Oh yeah, the kid," he said. "How's it going, Lare?" he asked. I took the case and the bottle from him and put them on the table, then shook the beefy hand he held out. I could tell by his breath and sleepy eyes that he'd been drinking for a while.

"Not too shabby," I answered. "Scoop?"

He eyed Johnny over my shoulder. "Just looking for a shaker."

"Well, there's the dance at the hall tonight."

"Naw," he said. "Can't. Got barred for being rowdy."

Juliet put her hand on Darcy's shoulder, and he limped back into the porch. His chunky ass under those sweat pants rippled. I turned and sat down. My armpits were dripping sweat and my knees were shaking. I was quite surprised I had stood up and done something.

"Man," I said. "That was close."

Johnny looked at me and said, "The hell was that all about?"

"That?" I answered. "Darcy gave me a concussion last year. I could have pressed charges but decided against it."

"Well, thanks for telling me." Johnny scoffed. "You and Thumper—bum buddies…"

"Johnny," I sliced, "if it wasn't for me, you two would be toe to toe right now, and I bet he'd be kicking your ass."

Johnny winced, so I continued. "You may have taken him in round one, but he's got some booze in him. Believe me, when he's drinking, he feels no pain. Right now I bet he's running on pure adrenaline. I seen him once take on two of the Mercier boys when he was loaded. He damn near kicked their heads in."

"Fuck."

"Yup," I said. "Now why do you call him Thumper?"

"That, little buddy," he said, "is something you'll hear about soon enough." Johnny messed up my hair and we watched some more TV. Juliet and Darcy talked for a long time on the porch. I was pretty scared that Darcy'd try something with Johnny, but at the same time I wanted to talk to him. I'd be a liar if I told you he didn't scare me, but something about guys like Darcy always intrigued me. I knew he had had his share of drugs, booze and fights. He was everything I wasn't. He was bad news, but still...

"Yo, Lare!" Darcy called out.

I went into the kitchen. Juliet walked past me, heading for Johnny. Darcy was standing by the stove and he waved me over. I noticed right away that the stove elements were bright red. My first thought was that he was going to burn me, the next that he wanted a tattoo, and third, that he wanted to get his ear pierced.

"You know what hot-knifing is?" he asked, holding two knives in his left hand and a beer in his right.

"No, Darce, can't say that I do."

"You ever do drugs before?"

"Nope."

"You wanna?" he said, a grin widening across his face.

Every fibre in my body, every molecule, every atom was screaming no, but instead I said, "Sure."

Van Halen boomed on the stereo and a light went out in the house.

"All right!!" he said, smiling like a Buddha. He slapped me on the back and reassured me that tonight was going to be great.

"Go into the bathroom and get me a roll of toilet paper."

I did. There was one roll with hardly any paper left on it, so I took that one. Darcy, upon seeing my pick, grunted, "Sure you ain't done this before?"

"Yup," I said. I noticed he had his knives propped in between the ribs of the red-hot elements. Their tips were glowing like horseshoes before the blacksmith hammers them into shape. I noticed some tin foil flattened out on the counter with a big chunk of black Plasticine in the centre of it and a whole bunch of baby Plasticines all around.

"Okay," Darcy said, "watch this." He pulled the knives out from the ribs of the elements and with his right blade touched one of the Plasticines. It stuck to the blade. He touched the left blade to the baby Plasticine and pressed the blades together. This hissed off a white smoke, which he puckered his lips for and inhaled.

The smell hit my nose and my eyes began to water.

Darcy held his breath and motioned for me to get the toilet paper roll.

"Okay, man," he said as he exhaled, "put your mouth over the end of the roll. Don't waste any…this is from Colombia, man… people died to get this to my main man in Hay River."

He did the same procedure with the baby Plasticines, touching the blades together at the other end of the toilet paper roll. The smoke went into my face, nose and mouth. Darcy put the knives down and covered my mouth and nose with his hands. I just about fainted; my knees wanted to buckle and my eyes were crying. The only thing that kept me standing was Darcy and his gorilla grip.

"Fuck, man, dontwasteitdontwasteitdontwasteit…," he commanded.

My lungs heaved and my throat was on fire. My hands were ripping at Darcy's and my eyes were wide open, looking at the ceiling. About twenty seconds later, Darcy decided I was allowed to breathe. I coughed and ran into the bathroom. I ran the water and drank about a gallon. When I looked in the mirror, I saw Darcy laughing.

"Weez brothers now," he giggled.

I wiped my eyes with a towel and said, "Let's do some more."

I hot-knifed about three more times. Never had I smelled or tasted anything so harsh. It felt like I was swallowing fire. I think more smoke went into my hair and eyes than anything. Darcy kept me in his famous "dontwasteit" grip. I felt normal at first and I thought that I would be invisible to the smoke, but then my blackouts began.

At first, it was like somebody had turned me off. I totally blanked out. When I woke up, I found myself sitting on the couch. The TV was off and Darcy, Johnny and Juliet were inches from my face, laughing and yelling. I could hear the Cult blaring from the stereo, "She Sells Sanctuary." I just sat there numb and happy.

"Hey, Lare," Johnny asked, "how do you feel?"

I wanted to say fine, but couldn't. All I could do was smile.

"Look," Darcy said, pointing to my smile. "He's got a permy."

They all laughed harder.

The next thing I knew, Darcy had a five-dollar bill in my face and was saying, "Goooo cliiiimb the telephoooone poooole outsiiiide."

I noticed Johnny and Juliet's laughter coming from the kitchen.

I looked straight into Darcy's eyes, straight in. I thought of all the things he could do to me but it came out anyway: "Fuck you, moose cock."

The next thing I knew, I was on the living room floor looking up at the crystal chandelier. Steve Perry's voice wailed about a small town girl taking the midnight train going anywhere. On the wall, Elvis was singing into his mike. All of the disciples looked towards Jesus.

For no reason whatsoever, I remembered this joke I had heard once. I couldn't remember how it went or who told it, but I stole the punch line and I started to say it. I started to moan, "Mommy, your monkey's eating Daddy's banana…" and then I started to wail, "Mother, your monkey's eating Daddy's banana…" and then I started to howl, "Mother, your monkey's eating Daddy's banana!"

After a while, I settled down and whispered, "I am my father's scream."

I guess I spooked everyone 'cause it sure got quiet. I looked out the window and I could see someone moving outside. I sat up and looked really hard into the frame. I could see a black man outside the window. He had a smile on his face from ear to ear and he was laughing at me. Shamus?

"Wait a minute," I thought, "just wait one goddamned minute." It was the Blue Monkeys of Corruption!

"Hey!" I yelled.

"Hey what?" Johnny yelled back.

"Time is it?" I yelled.

"Quarter to nine. What's wrong?"

"Get the Blue Monkeys the hell out of here!"

"Who?"

"Blue Monkeys! You know, from India. They're missing their hands and arms. They're after the hash, man. They want the smoke!"

"Get off the dope, man!" Johnny yelled and I could hear laughing.

"No more!" I pleaded. "No more!" I was so scared that it got funny. Don't ask me why, but I laughed until I was crying and then I laughed some more.

"Hey!" I yelled.

"Hey what?" Juliet yelled back.

"Time is it?"

"Five to nine."

I thought an hour had passed. I laughed harder than the first time. The monkeys disappeared.

The next thing I knew I was sprawled out on the kitchen floor watching Johnny and Juliet kissing. AC/DC was on the system roaring on about the highway to Hell. Johnny had her on the kitchen counter. He was standing and her legs were wrapped around him. They still had their clothes on and Juliet was running her hands through Johnny's hair. I knew something magical was in the air. Johnny knew I was watching and kept winking at me. I didn't have the giggles but I just couldn't stop staring. It was like a movie, only real.

"Let's go check on the kids," Juliet said. "I gotta go check on the kids."

Then I blacked out and found myself in the bathroom. I was inches away from the mirror. I was looking into my eyes, trying to catch my pupils dilate as I turned the lights off and on, off and on. The door was closed and I was alone.

That was when I heard the water bed in the next room.

First I heard the slish slish slish and the stirring of bubbles and then I heard Juliet. Her breathing was heavy and excited.

I hopped into the bathtub and pressed my ear into the wall. I wanted to hear everything. My socks were wet and my head was ringing but I just had to hear Juliet.

The water bed became frantic. The wood frame was hitting the nearest wall and I could hear Juliet's voice, the sweetest voice I have ever heard. It was a gentle shiver, the edge of a whisper, the tender shake of a leaf, it was now, here, and she was panting, "Oh Johnny, oh Johnny, come on, come on."

She went on and on. I was so alive listening to them. My heart was pounding and my blood was pumping. *Juliet. Juliet.* I started to fill my mouth with water from the tap.

"JULIET!" a voice boomed out.

There was a thunderous pounding on the door that shook the house, shook the room, shook my little black soul. My first thought: My mother has come to castrate me. My second: Jesus has come to collect. And my third: It's the cops!

"Juliet, you're supposed to be watching the children. Get your clothes on and get out here!"

I froze. All I knew was that it was a woman's voice and that I was in the bathtub stoned and hard. My mind was going a million miles an hour. I was a rabbit, choking in a snare. I was falling through ice. I was slamming the hammer down on my father. I was—

The pounding got louder.

"Juliet—now!"

I heard the water bed sloshing and Johnny tripping.

"Shit," he whispered.

I heard the door open and Johnny step out into the hallway.

"Who the hell are you?" the voice yelled.

No answer. I heard Johnny walk down into the kitchen and into the porch.

"You stay right there, Mister! I'm going to have the cops down here in two minutes…"

Still no answer from Johnny. Now he started calling my name, wondering where I was.

"Larry? Lare? Larry?" I could tell he was heading outside.

"You get your ass back in here," the voice called out the door.

"Fuck you!" he called back.

I got out of the tub and stopped at the door.

"Shitshitshitshit." Panic. Total and absolute panic. My eyes bulged and my balls sucked back into my belly. I hunched and squinted, prepared for a beating. Who the hell was out there and why were they after me? What did they want with Juliet and

Johnny? I just about pissed my pants. I got brave; I opened the door. There was no one there. I walked past the door to the bedroom Johnny had come out of. I looked in as I walked by.

I saw Juliet.

Juliet was sitting on the bed looking at me. Her shirt was off and I could see her breasts. I wanted to look but couldn't. I couldn't pull myself from those sad, sad eyes. It was like something was broken inside. It was like I had listened to something that wasn't supposed to happen.

I stuttered a good-bye.

She didn't answer. She just kept staring at me. She had the eyes of a fawn shot in mid-leap. The Blue Monkeys of Corruption laughed and howled, putting the rifle down. And like my mother's gaze, I realized what it meant:

Slaughter.

I was the beast.

I was close to the beast.

He was running beside me.

I could hear the hoofs scrape against the pavement before the deliverance kick to a swelling face.

And there were scorch marks on the road where we danced.

Someone was screaming at me to kick

to scrape a face raw

the skin and slaughter

to sniff again

to scrape again through the window

to hear my cousins pop and burn

shards of glass in my back

screaming glass

to see my father fuck—

"Who in the hell are you?" the voice boomed. I jumped and turned to meet it.

IT WAS JULIET'S MOM!

I froze, my eyes wide.

Mrs. Hope looked me over. She put her hand on her hip. "You're Verna's boy, ain't ya?"

"Yes, ma'am," I said. I could hear Johnny outside still calling my name. I stammered for explanations. Everything was moving so fast. I walked past her and into the porch. The door was open and I could see Johnny. He was putting his shirt on and he had our shoes in his hands. He motioned for me to get my ass over there.

"You little bastards!" Juliet's mom called out after me. "I'm going to call the police."

"Whoopdeefuckindoo!" Johnny called back, laughing, "the cops!"

"Yeah!" I hollered. "Yeah, ya fuckinbitchcow!"

Johnny looked at me puzzled and mouthed, "Fuckin' bitch cow?"

"I'm going to have Social Services here in two minutes!" Missus Hope called from the porch.

"Hoooly fuuuck!" Johnny and I yelled together and we began to run. We ran down the paved roads in our socks. The ground was cold and I started laughing. Johnny started laughing too, and he handed me my shoes. I suppose we could have stopped to put them on, but it just seemed hilarious running down the back roads of town. We were sprinting and laughing, yelling and out of breath by the time we cut through the potato fields down by our street. We ended up by the track outside the high school. My lungs were burning and I was wide awake. My socks were still wet, caked with dirt and slush. I wasn't buzzing any more, but I sure was anxious to hear what Johnny had to say.

"That was close," he said as he put on his shoe. He was tipsy, so I let him use my arm for support. He was still giggling a bit, looking down. "Manohman, what a night. You get stoned, I get laid, we're all happy and the cops are out looking for us."

My feet were freezing. "Don't forget Social Services, too," I added, looking over my shoulder.

I didn't think Missus Hope would call the cops. But I was scared she'd call my mom. Man, I'd die if my mom found out. I'd just die.

I laced up my shoes. "What'd you guys do?"

Johnny laughed again. "Oh come on, Lare, I made her and she made me. We had sex, skronked, humped, penetrated souls. We fucked!"

"What's it like?" I asked. My mouth betrayed me. I wanted to take it back and act like I knew. But Johnny didn't seem to notice. He straightened up and took a step forward. He leaned into my face and said, "A bit too bony for me. She did this thing with her hips when she was riding me...man, that hurt. But other than that she was okay."

"Did you use a condom?"

"Fuck no," he said, "and if she gives me the clap, I'll kill her."

"Well, maybe you should take a shower or something," I stammered. What a fuckin' thing to say about Juliet. I remembered sex education and what the doctor had said: Fort Simmer is the STD capital of the Territories. He said that a shower would get rid of some of the bacteria.

"I got a system," Johnny whispered. "I use a toothpick."

"WHAT?!"

"I stick it in the tip of my dick and scoop out all the jupe. That way no little disease gets me. No burning sensation when I urinate, no cheezy white discharge...you know, no pissing fire."

"Wow," I said. "That's pretty smart." (For a fuckin' asshole)

"Damn straight!" he boasted. "Invented that little technique myself."

"Right on." (Fuck off)

We paused for a moment and I think it may have registered what had happened. Somewhere in the world, we had made the

54

nervous fingers of rain explode into the white palm of snow, but here, in Fort Simmer, I could no longer see the Jesus in Johnny. We walked. Johnny said he had to go home and get some sleep "after the toothpick did its magic." I nodded and walked home alone. I snuck into the house quietly. I didn't even take off my jacket. I went into my room, undressed and went straight to bed.

It was about twenty minutes later when the phone rang. I snatched it up so my mom wouldn't get it. Who was it? Social Services? Juliet's mom ? The cops?

"Lare!" Johnny yelled.

"What?" I whispered. He had AC/DC blasting and he yelled, "The Big Kahoona wants to know who the fuck the blue monkeys are and what the hell was that with 'Ya fuckin' bitch cow.'"

I heard him laughing before he hung up. What a guy!

Jazz

ONCE I HAD Johnny for a friend, I didn't hang around home much, just to say hi and do chores. My mom didn't seem to mind. She was studying a lot for her tests and we pretty well came and went as we pleased. She was happy 'cause Jed was coming to town and that was fine with me. I liked hanging around Johnny. He took good care of me.

There was this guy named Jazz at school. Jazz had failed a lot of grades, and he always used to make fun of me. It got so I'd be just about crying 'cause he was so brutal. I hate it when people laugh at me, and Jazz was the goddamned messiah when it came to making people laugh.

The only thing I can compare Jazz to is a jackal. He had a skinny little ass and no body fat. When he took his shirt off in gym class, it looked like he'd been pulled inside out. He could play the spoons on his six-pack. He had buck teeth and dark black eyes. He had black straw hair and always wore caps, usually ones that said "Arctic Cat" or "Polaris." He wore Montreal Canadiens sweat bands around his wrists, and he had these skinny sharp knuckles that he rapped the desks with, usually acting cool, doing a drum solo. From what I'd heard, he'd always been an asshole. This guy called Rob Dupe told me that when Jazz was a kid in elementary, his folks couldn't afford running shoes for him, so what he'd do was he'd go barefoot. He used to lick the bottom of his feet for traction, and he'd run laps all over the damn place. He was fast, too. Every few laps he'd stop, brush off his feet, lick 'em for traction and go at it some more.

Jazz used to tease me 'cause I'm pretty visibly native. "So, Larry," he'd say, "you like the Arctic, eh?"

"Yeah," I'd mumble. (You fuckin' foot-licker)

Then he'd lean into me and say, "You zug-zug little girls to keep warm, eh?"

And everyone would laugh.

"Hey, Dogrib," he'd say. I don't know how he found out about me being Dogrib. I guess it was from his mom. She liked to gossip.

"They're having a sale on Lysol down the street. I seen your mom passed out in a ditch. I fucked her for fifteen bucks."

Man, it hurt to hear him say things like that. I know Mister Harris heard him too, but he never did a thing. Jazz had pushed a teacher through a pane of glass a few years ago, and he'd been cocky ever since. I was a nervous wreck each day before class, and I guess Johnny kinda caught on.

One day we were on a field trip to the Northern Lights Museum. Our whole home room was allowed to go because this Micmac writer, Lorne Simon, was in town reading some of his stuff. Mostly we went to these things just to get the hell out of school. I was walking by myself, and Jazz walked up behind me. He had his giggle gang with him and he started in on me. I couldn't see any teachers or anyone around who could help me.

"Lysol Larry, I got some warm piss for you to drink. You Indians drink anything, doncha? I got a forty-ouncer with a worm at the bottom. Bite the worm, Larry," he said, and grabbed his crotch. I blushed and walked faster. He grabbed me from behind and said, "You gonna turn away from me, faggot? You gonna turn away from me?"

I could tell he was gonna slap me and I could tell he knew I knew. I just stood there. I guess my eyes were wide and he started to smile. He was winding up to crack me when a voice cut through the air.

"Jazz, you're like a shit that just won't flush."

"What?" Jazz roared and turned around. Johnny stood there with a smoke in his mouth, looking right into Jazz.

"Fuck off," Johnny said, "or I'll kick a bone outta your ass."

Nobody moved. Jazz looked at his friends for help but everybody looked away. Johnny shot out and smacked Jazz hard on the face. Jazz's hair whipped around as he fell, and he stayed down.

"Come on, cocksucker," Johnny growled, "get up."

Jazz and his skinny little ass stayed down and Johnny watched him for a while. My face was burning. I started to walk away.

I could hear Johnny's runners spitting up gravel as he ran up behind me.

"Hey, Lare," he said. "Why do Canadian couples like to hump doggy-style?"

"I dunno." I started to smile. "Why?"

"So they can both watch *Hockey Night in Canada*!" he yelled, and that was that. We laughed, and he slapped me on the back.

"It's okay, man," he said, looking back at Jazz. "A turd never gets too far from the toilet bowl."

Kiss

I SMOKED UP a lot after that first night. Sometimes it was in the potato field; other times it was at Johnny's apartment. We had to be careful of Donny. He was a bandit.

"Hey, chief," he said as he walked into the kitchen. "I got a quarter that says you don't have hair on your nuts."

"What?" I asked in disbelief. Johnny was in the bathroom so it was just Donny and me. Van Halen was playing on the stereo and it was a Friday.

"You heard me, chief," he said. "We on, or are you a baldy?"

"Hey, Donny," I said, motioning towards the swear jar, "you better cool it. You're headed for a burn out."

"Whatever," he sneered as he sat across from me. "Wanna play some cards? I know crib, rummy, crazy eights, crazy eight count down. You know crazy eight countdown? Here, I'll show you."

Just as he was about to start dealing, I noticed a small hole in his left hand. It wasn't big. It looked like a dent.

"Hey," I asked and touched his hand. "What happened?"

"Oh," he said.

"Scoop?"

Donny looked down and covered the hole. He said in a whisper, "A man at one of my mom's parties put a cigarette out on my hand."

"Oh, man, I'm sorry—"

Johnny came around the corner tucking in his shirt.

"Donny," he pleaded, "I told you no more cards. Did you do your homework?"

"Awww, it's stupid," he answered."As if I'm going to use that stuff anyway."

"Come on, Donny," he answered, "your report card said—"

"Dad said I didn't have to if I didn't want to."

Johnny stood over him and started pointing. He raised his voice. "You don't listen to him, okay? You listen to me. The only thing you have to worry about right now is how you're gonna raise those marks!"

Donny's face started to darken and he folded his arms.

"Understand?" Johnny asked.

Donny didn't answer, and I got embarrassed for him.

"Jeeeez," Donny said. "Okay then…"

"I know it sucks but you gotta do it," Johnny said. "Dad's coming soon. We're almost out of this shit town. Now go in your room and do some homework, okay?"

"But I want to talk with Larry," he answered.

I smiled.

"Larry's gonna be here for a while. You do that homework and you can talk to him after."

"Yeah?" he asked.

"Yeah," I answered.

Donny got up and walked into his room. "Turn the music down," he called over his shoulder.

Johnny got up and went into the living room. He turned the music down and came back. "Man, what am I gonna do about that kid? Did you see his teeth? They're already yellow."

I was still in shock over Donny's hand. "How bad is it at school?" I asked.

"Pretty bad. I got his report card and he's got a lot of C's and a few D's. I went and talked to his teacher and she said he's a wise guy in class who likes to fight."

"Hmmm," I said."What does your mom think?"

"Mom doesn't give a shit," Johnny answered. I kept my mouth shut.

Johnny put his hands together like he was praying and exhaled loudly. He closed his eyes and I watched him.

"How's your coffee?" he said after a minute.

"Donkey piss," I said. "Weak."

"Yeah, yeah, we're running low."

Johnny's hair had fallen over his forehead. He was handsome, but in a lost sort of way. He could grow a beard if he wanted to and some days he didn't shave. Sometimes when we were stoned I'd see him staring at me with those glittering blue eyes of his.

"If I could perform the autopsy on him," I thought, "I'd steal his eyes."

I got up and went to the stereo. "Hey! Let's write a song. We'll call it 'Hickey Juice.'"

"Yeah," he called back, "the first line will be, 'She's a little bitch with a capital B!'"

I shook my head and smiled. We were listening to Van Halen. The synthesizer and drums were pounding "I'll Wait until Your Love Comes Down." I turned it up just a bit while Johnny fired up the hot knives on the stove in the kitchen. He peeked around the corner and smiled. "Landlord's gonna shit!"

"Piss on 'im!" I yelled. I was on the couch, having another coffee. I was downing coffee about five times a day. The cool thing about Johnny's place was they drank coffee out of glass mugs. I always felt like a trucker on Highway 5, taking a break in some diner in South Dakota, taking sips from my glass mug, having a smoke, my rough scraggy beard on my face, my wallet thick with fifties.

I started thinking about Juliet. I really had this thing for her—I'm talking twelve cylinders of love! I mean, my nipples became fire ants at the thought of her: red, hard and venomous. I could close my eyes and see her, and when I did it was like somebody pulled my heart a little. She got grounded for what happened at the party and tonight was her first night of freedom. I know. I marked it on my calendar.

Johnny told me tons about his past. He had a slew of pictures of pretty girls. Mostly he went for brunettes. In lots of the pictures, they had purple hickeys on their necks and bottles in their hands. I was always hoping that he'd open up about Juliet and tell me more about what she was like, what she did, how she did it. I had brought this "Best of Iron Maiden" tape over that I had mixed. Man, the music felt good. "Wasted Years" was blaring now, and if it weren't for Donny, we'd have had it cranked even higher. Johnny came around the corner from the kitchen and gave me thumbs-up. I joined him and inhaled the hash. No hooter this time. Just me and the smoke.

"Yeah," I thought, "the day I saw Juliet Hope was the day I felt my pubic hair grow." I could still close my eyes and see her on the bed. I looked at Johnny, who was at the table rolling a fatty.

"You know, Lare, I had this girl once, her name was Lisa Beatty. What a fuck doll. This one time we were fooling around and she gave me a hickey. I told her not to do it again, and she did. She gave me another one and I got her back. I gave her hickeys on her ass. I did a big J on one cheek and a big B on the other. She was a lifeguard at the swimming pool in Hay River, and she had this bathing suit that was green and white. When she dove into the water, you could see the J and B—and I wasn't the only one who noticed!"

"Wow!" I said. "Now that's a story!"

"Yeah," he smiled, "that's Hay River for you. She was smooth, brother, smooth."

"Wasted Years" ended; "Power Slave" began. We paused to listen to the guitars. The glasses on the table were shaking as I inhaled some more.

I sat down next to Johnny and put my hand on his shoulder. He looked at me and I smiled. I had never really said anything to him about helping me out, and now it seemed like I could say it without sounding like a pansy. "Thanks for taking care of Jazz, man."

Johnny smiled back. "No prob." He thought about it as he rolled. "Listen, Lare, I gotta teach you some new moves."

"Yeah?" I asked. "Yeah, you better. I don't know how to fight."

"The next time you smoke someone it better be three hits: you hitting them, the shit hitting their shorts and the ambulance hitting ninety!"

I laughed.

"Stand up and put your arms on my shoulders."

I did.

He whipped his arms over mine and slapped them around my back. He pulled up while he kneed me in the gut.

"Ugh," I grunted and hit the floor.

"Lare," he laughed, "you gotta block it."

I struggled up and rested on bent knees. I guess he could see that I was mad because he sat down again and straightened his hair with his hands. I could smell the Right Guard in his scalp. He had showed me that if you sprayed your head with it for a long time, you could do cartwheels and your hair wouldn't move. Rubbing my gut, I stared at him.

"So tell me about being full blood," he said. I sat down. "Whattaya wanta know?"

He got up and handed me a cigarette. He was saving the joints till later.

"Well, what tribe are you? Chip? Cree?"

"Dogrib."

"I thought they were from around Yellowknife."

I got a little nervous. "Yeah."

"What's the scoop?"

"Well, Jed told me that our tribe came from a woman who

gave birth to six puppies." I eyed him while I said that because I knew some people would laugh. He didn't, so I continued.

"Well, she had to live by herself in the woods so she could raise her pups. One day she left her hut so she could check her snares, and when she came home she could see human footprints in the snow and ashes."

"No shit," Johnny said.

"Yeah...so one day she went out like she was going to check her snares but she snuck back and watched her hut. She could hear her pups yapping like this: Yap! Yap! Then she could hear them laughing like children. After a while she could hear kids running around the hut and choo! Out from the hut run six kids, all naked."

"Whoah!"Johnny said.

"Yeah! So she watches them and they're playing in the snow all laughing and having a great time. She runs out of the bush and chases them back into the hut. They all make a run for the bag she used to leave them in. Three make it and turn back to pups. A girl and two boys don't. She catches them. They stay human and they're the first Dogribs. She raised them to be beautiful hunters with strong medicine."

"Hunh. Wait a minute," Johnny interrupted. "What happened to the three that made it back to the bag?"

"Humph. I don't know. Jed never told me that part."

"Better find out."

We were quiet for a bit. Then he spoke.

"Lare, that's something. That's really something. You're a storyteller, man. Your voice even changed when you talked."

"Yeah?" I asked, proud of the moment and the revelation. That was the first time I had told the story and I liked how it felt.

"Larry?" Johnny said. "Do you drink?"

"Oh," I said, "I had a bet going with my dad that I wouldn't touch a drop of liquor until I turned eighteen. He said he'd give me a hundred bucks if I make it."

"Where is your dad?" he asked.

"Oh…uh, I don't know. He and my mom split up. It was a bad scene."

"Yeah," he said, "I know what you mean. Shit city, hey?"

"Hunh," I agreed. "How come you?"

"Long story, man. It sucks the cockaruski."

"Aaah, come on."

"I'll say this," he said. "I have a feeling if I picked up a bottle, I'd never put it down."

I nodded. "Deep."

"It's casual, man. You only bet a hundred dollars with your old man?"

"I was nine when I made that bet. At the time, a hundred bucks was a hunk of a hunk."

"Sounds good. I should get that deal going with Donny."

Johnny lit a joint and handed it to me, looking at my lips. I got nervous, so I asked, "What do you think of Miss Sauvé's tits?"

"Don't matter to me," he winked. "The kind of fucking I do, you don't need tits."

I started to laugh, and he pointed to my lips. "Time for a shave."

"What?"

"Time for a shave there, muskrat mouth. You look like Charles Manson."

"You figure?"

"Yeah, look. Juliet's coming over in a bit. You better shave before she gets here. Maybe she'll bring a friend. Go in the bathroom and shave that fuzz off your lip."

"I never shaved before."

"Well, it ain't that hard. Go on!"

I felt the whiskers on my lip and agreed. I walked to his bathroom. "Use my electric!" he yelled. I locked the door and saw dirty towels, toothpaste spitting out of the tube and yellowed Q-Tips lying on the counter.

The doors under the sink were hard to open so I yanked. They gave. It was the weirdest thing; behind some blue Tampax boxes and rolls of toilet paper, I saw some bottles. I moved the boxes aside, and there were two big-ass bottles of Golden Wedding.

"Holy shit," I whispered. What if Donny got a hold of these?

I thought of Johnny saying, "That's one woman you'll never want to meet" about his mom. Looking at those two bottles, I suddenly knew why.

"House of Pain" began on the stereo. I was a bit nervous because of what I had found. I shut the cupboard door and continued with my search. I couldn't find an electric razor, so I used a pink one lying on the side of the tub. I could hear the buzzer go off in the hallway. That meant that someone was downstairs in the lobby and wanted to come up. I ran the water and squirted some shaving cream into my hand. I put the lather on my lips, under my nose, on my cheek and in my sideburns. I grabbed the razor. Resting it on my chin, I yanked up, just like in the movies, and sliced my nostril.

"Shit!" I hissed. I started bleeding in the cream. I pushed down on the blade the next time for traction and I screamed some more. Shit! What was I doing wrong? The next time, I pulled the razor down my lip. That seemed to be smoother. I shaved my sideburns too, and then I dried my face on a white towel, leaving a blur of blood behind. I looked into the mirror. My upper lip was red and blotchy, and it was swelling up like a worm about ready to burst. My sideburns itched and my face was starting to feel like it was on fire. I put some after-shave on. My face burned even more, and I whimpered like a puppy. The music stopped, and I heard Johnny start it up again. I looked at myself again in the mirror.

"Shit," I said. "Juliet."

I didn't want her to see me bleeding to death so I knocked on Donny's door.

"Enter," he said. I did.

Donny's room was pretty barren. All he had was a box spring, a mattress and a lamp. He was sitting on the carpet, drawing.

"Whatcha doing?"

"What's it look like, chief?" he said, holding up his picture.

It was bizarre. There was a kid holding a gun and he was smiling; in the background there were five dogs lying dead, with a hundred lines behind them saying the same thing: "Stab the dog stab the dog stab the dog."

"Whatdaya think, chief?" His eyes were looking into me for a reaction, so I told the truth.

"Pretty grim."

He snatched it back. "Yeah, what do you know?"

As I looked around, I realized he had drawings hung up all over. In the bare closet he had drawn on the wall. There were men and women crying and there were fallen-down scarecrows, thousands of them. He had tried to write swear words, but they all came out like, "Fok FoK fOK."

"Shit, man, you psycho?"

"Gotta be. It's a fuckin' war zone," he said.

"You're rude."

"I guess," he said and looked down.

"It snowed," I offered.

"Big deal. Snow melts."

"No," I said, "you should be playing outside."

"And freeze?"

We were quiet.

"You know," I tried. "I was reading that playing Mozart helps plants grow."

He went back to drawing. "Fuck Mozart."

"Sol later, man," I said.

"Yeah, sol, chief."

Aha! At least somebody knew some Raven Talk.

I walked down the hallway, and the synthesizer shot Van Halen's "1984" into my veins. I got piss shivers. I heard the clink of bottles and laughter. I went around the corner and there she was: Juliet.

But she was with Jazz! Jakka Jazz! The biggest asshole in the universe! The Leonard of all Leonards! I looked at Johnny, but Juliet and him were hugging and kissing, slopping their tongues all over each other. Johnny had his hands in her hair and she was grabbing him back.

"Were you pushing or pulling in there?" Jazz asked me. Johnny's giving him a lickin' hadn't changed anything at all.

"What?" I slurred. That music was too loud. I could see Juliet laughing at me and my fat lips. I could see Johnny squinting at me, and I felt humiliated. Everyone was laughing and I hated it. I could see Juliet's ass in those black pants that I loved. I could see Jazz and his smug skinny-ass face. He was drinking out of my favourite glass mug and he had beer in it. I could see Johnny giving me the knee and I could hear the hoofs on the pavement again and I could hear the puppy being torn to pieces and dogs roaring. The whole damn world was turning up the volume. I could see the nurses who made me look in the mirror and me screaming when I saw the skin peeling from my cousins as the people pulled the blankets off; and my father doing it—my father fucking, the teeth of the hammer sinking into his soft eyes and me yelling, "I send you to hell, Daddy, I send you to hell!"

"I said!" Jazz reached out and pinched my nose. "Were you pushing or pulling in the bathroom—"

I punched Jazz so damn hard his feet touched the ceiling. He hit the floor rolling and I landed on top of him. I was yelling so loud I couldn't hear the music. Johnny pulled me off him after a bit. I guess he knew Jazz had it coming. I felt like I had water in my lungs. I couldn't breathe. I just couldn't take it. I tried to put my fist through Jazz so hard that I heard something snap. After that, I blacked out.

Next thing I knew, I was on the couch. Johnny and Juliet were looking at me. Juliet's eyes were huge as she put a blanket over me.

"Holy shit, Larry," she said. "If you were Mexican you'd be Rocky!"

"Larry, holy fuck."Johnny shook his head and offered me a smoke. "You didn't have to do that, man. You busted his nose!"

I waved the smoke away and looked at Juliet. I savoured her hair. It looked like a fire on a mountain rolling down into the forest. She was chewing gum: Bubblicious. I could smell that it was strawberry flavour. I wanted that gum so bad. I saw the glint of her teeth and I wanted her. Big time.

"Gimme gum," I said, and she gave it to me. She stuck it in my mouth and I bit soft. Johnny took her other hand and led her away. I watched them as they went around the corner. I heard a door close. The music had changed. This time it was Power Station: "Get it on! Bang a gong!"

I got up and sat at the kitchen table. I was looking at my swollen knuckles. The blood from Jazz's nose had caked on them and turned chocolate brown. There was blood on my white socks. I could see cigarette butts in an ashtray, one with Juliet's lipstick on it. I picked it up. It was a small butt and I lit it. I placed my lips where she had placed hers. I puckered and swallowed deep. I burned my thumb and lip; I coughed and hacked. The music had ended, so I put Van Halen back on. I turned it low and sat down. I looked out the window and tried pretty hard not to look at my reflection. When I heard the bed bang chang against the wall, I turned up the system as loud as it would go.

I had it bad for Juliet. I wanted her for my secret, my prayer. I wanted her as my sweet violence of seeds and metal. I wanted to spill candles with her, to hold hands and walk around in gumboots with her. I wanted to do anything and everything with her. I mean, if she were in a coma, I'd make sure the nurses played her favourite music over and over so she'd come back to life and thank me.

I was looking at the floor, past my bloody socks, and I saw those burns in the linoleum floor, the ones that looked like scorched blurred eyes. Except this time it wasn't the ceiling they were staring at: it was me. They were studying me and I wondered what they were seeing, what they were thinking.

I sat back on the couch, and all I could do was think of when I was younger. I looked around the living room. There was a couch like this one in the old house, but ours was green. The music was blasting then, too. My dad stood over my mom. He had called me out of my room. He was holding the yellow broom. He was speaking French. He had learned it in the residential schools. He never talked about what had happened there, but he always talked French when he drank.

My mom was passed out on the couch. A couch like this one. This was back when she used to drink. She had gone to residential schools, too. She was passed out, in her bathrobe. My father took the broom stick and started laughing. He spread her legs and with the yellow broomstick—

I shot awake.

"Fuck fuck fuck," I said. "No!"

I purposely made myself remember the lake in Rae. One time

before the accident, I was hanging out with my cousins there. We used to play in the sand way down the beach. We'd take some toys down and build houses. We'd also sniff gas. I wasn't too crazy about it at first, but after seeing my dad do the bad thing to my aunt, it took the shakes away. I could feel the heat on my back from the sun. Every now and then we'd stop to eat or take a leak. Me and my cousin Franky were good pals, even though he was demented. He was the guy who told me that if you touch gasoline to a cat's asshole, the cat'd jump ten feet into the air. He was the guy who taught me about bennies.

He'd say, "Close your eyes, Larry. Close them tight. Now face the sun, that's right. Face it and feel the bennies bouncing off you."

I'd close my eyes so tight my forehead would stretch, and after a while I'd relax and, sure enough, I could feel bennies bouncing off me. They'd hit one area and the warmth would spread. It was glorious. I began to shout, "Hey! Hey, Franky! I feel them! I feel them!"

One time we were taking leaks and facing the sun. We could feel the bennies bouncing off us and we were yelling, "Bennies! Bennies! Bennies!" but soon I was the only one who was yelling, and when I opened my eyes, there was Franky pointing at my feet.

"Cousin," he whispered, "you're pissing blood." I was.

That's all I remember.

I woke up when Johnny led Juliet to the door. She was putting on her running shoes and her damn sweater was inside out. Why didn't she just goddamned advertise on the blue channel: "Hello! I just got plowed!"

She had her damn socks off and I could see her tiny toes. I wanted to run over there and bite her ass! Johnny kissed her and told her he'd call her. She hugged him and whispered something to him. He laughed. After she left, he came over and sat next to me. His hair was messed up and he didn't look too happy either.

"Lare," he asked, "what's in your hair?"

I didn't answer. I just looked at him. I knew he was gonna give me a lecture.

"Let's go for a walk," he said.

Floaters

FORT SIMMER BRACES for two things in winter. The first is the cold. The second is the Floaters. Floaters are the town drunks who stagger around the community at all hours of the night. Hobo Jungle is where they camp. But when it's cold out, they come into town to pass out in the alleys, or in the hotel lobby or at the taxi stand. Some throw bricks through the windows of the Bay so they can be charged and shipped off to Yellowknife where they can hibernate and clean up. They are the lost, and Johnny and I walked among them. The ice popped and cracked under our feet and we shimmied like we were wearing kimonos.

Johnny took me out to the back roads of town, by the landslide. We passed two men, one of whom shuffled slow with his head down; the other jumped around him, shadowboxing in old tennis shoes and a bright yellow sweater. His big belly bounced up and down, and he strutted up to us, away from his brother.

"I'm a boxer!" he said and raised his fists. His breath rose above him and plumed like a baby Hiroshima.

The other man was trying to say something in his raspy voice. He was drunk. I could smell the men downwind. They reeked of sweet Lysol and sour fish. The raspy man's voice was haunting, as if he were a face screaming without a throat.

"Have you ever walked in the footsteps of Jesus?" he asked. I

71

could see his long nose, which slid across his face like a snake off its trail. It had been broken many times. His eyes were black, as black as the eyes of a corpse. They were lifeless, staring at me.

"No," I said.

Rasp Man shambled closer and raised his hands like the lord of the cross. "Have you ever walked in the footsteps of Satan?" he whispered. I stepped back instinctively. I did not want to touch the man or breathe the air around him.

"Great!" Johnny said and came between the Boxer and his brother. He handed the Boxer a smoke. The man stopped his fists long enough to accept it. Johnny lit it for him. Rasp Man floated towards them. I couldn't see his feet move. He just floated. I heard a quiet thanks that sounded like a death prayer and both men shook Johnny's hand. Johnny said something to them and they continued on their way towards town. Johnny put his hands in his pockets and walked over to me.

"Fuckin' chronics," he whispered.

I was cold and shivering. We started following the brothers towards the town lights. There were pockets of snow on the roads and the ice had glassed over in a thick skin. When the Floaters walked on the ice, it cracked, sounding like panes of glass.

"You really did it tonight, buddy," Johnny said, changing his tone. "Now you're in. Now you gotta learn the rules of fighting. When you broke Jazz's nose—and you owe me one for wiping up the blood—you got brought into a circle. This circle is one for fighters, like Buddy X up there," he motioned with his head.

The bigger man was shadowboxing his fists about his brother's head without making contact. He was quick. His belly bounced and bounced. Rasp Man cackled back and started to call and cough loudly. It was a scene of shadow puppets, almost as if we were watching an ape and a lizard meet in an arena. Rasp Man raised his arms again and the Boxer held him.

Johnny snorted and lit up a smoke. "Pretty soon the word is gonna be out that you're a scrapper. The next time you're at a party and someone's looking for a fight they might grab you. You're fair game now. You're in."

He took a puff and passed the cigarette to me. I was smiling inside: I was in.

"This here's unspoken. I'm only gonna say it once. If you get into a fight and you get hurt bad, stay down. Just stay down and cover your head. Whoever it is that's scrapping you will take that as a surrender. It works 99 per cent of the time. If they're drunk, you just run your Indian ass the hell out of there, 'cause drunks like to keep kicking. If they're stoned, they'll usually stop when you cover your head. You got that?"

I took a drag and handed the smoke back to him. "Yeah," I said, "go on."

The brothers stopped up ahead. They were arguing. The Boxer started to yell and Johnny and I stopped to watch. There weren't any streetlights where we were, but the men were close enough to the Bay that we could make out their silhouettes. The Boxer planted his feet in the cold gravel. The raspy brother tried to walk away, but was grabbed and shaken by the Boxer. Johnny continued to talk, keeping a watchful eye on the two men.

"Larry," he said, "if I have to listen to my mom fuck one more guy, I don't know what I'm gonna do."

He went silent, and I felt sad.

"Johnny," I said. "I didn't know…"

"Well, shit," he said, blowing smoke in my face, "now you got the hunger; you'll probably want to start screwing anything that walks. I'll tell you something, Lare, and this is coming to you straight. Sex is a drug; once you start, you can't stop. Sometimes it's downright ugly what people will do to get it."

"Man, I know that," I said, thinking of my father.

Up ahead, Rasp Man was trying to get free of the Boxer. His hands fluttered like the wings of a shot chicken. The Boxer yelled into his face and shook him again. In the distance, from where I stood, they looked like lovers in an incredible dance.

Johnny continued with his grim message. "You wanna start screwing someone, you talk to Dean Meddows. His mom works at the hospital as a nurse. She knows all the girls in this town that have the dose. She tells Dean every name. I know it's bad—you can just close your mouth—but this is a shit town and she's just looking out for her own. I had Juliet checked out. She's okay. You think you'll remember that before you wet your wick? You pay Dean five bucks and he'll give you a list of all the chicks who got the clap."

"Yeah," I said, watching the brothers. Johnny took a long drag and handed me the smoke. "What else?"

The Boxer threw his brother on the ground and proceeded to smash his sneakers into him. The younger man began to scream. I started to run towards them, but Johnny grabbed my jean jacket and held me with sudden tank force.

"Never fuck a friend," he said, looking into my eyes. "That's the golden rule."

I looked back towards the two men. "They're ghosts, Johnny."

"Wha?"

"Nobody's told them they died." I took a big sallow. "Nobody told them they're dead."

Big Daddy Love in Free Fall

JOHNNY AND I had been walking for a while when we came to the church. Johnny howled to the moon, and I could hear the scrape of claws on steel as a thousand ravens on the church roof steadied themselves in the wind. I thought to myself, "This is how death must feel, with its claws cold and sinking."

The ravens snapped their black razor bills like a million crabs in battle. I couldn't see the ravens but I bet they were sharpening their beaks and watching us, their life-steam rising like a thousand tangled arms. Johnny was walking ahead of me. I started to talk to myself so that anything out there would know we were coming. I just gave in to what I felt and started to free-fall inside. I guess I was babbling for quite a while, 'cause when Johnny stopped suddenly I bumped into him.

"What's that?" Johnny asked. "What'd you say?"

"What?"

"You were singing."

"I was?" I felt so incredibly tired and wanted to go home.

"Yeah, you kept singing, 'In her tongue is the law of kindness, in her tongue is the law of kindness.'"

"It's from the Bible. I can't remember where."

"You said Ewoks looked like burn victims. You said you hated their teeth."

"Guess I'm just tired."

"You guess? Man, you're something else, you know that?"

"Whatever," I said.

"You don't remember any of this, do you?"

"No."

"You said the devil lives in a church."

"That's what they say."

"That's fuckin' freaky, man. Explain that."

I thought of my father. "Can't say."

"Shit, man. You're a poet or something."

Then why can't I have Juliet? I wanted to ask.

We went back to Johnny's apartment and I collapsed on the

couch. I dreamed that night of stunt men doing cartwheels with dry assholes, ripping themselves in half, and ravens, all the ravens watching, their beaks spread, open.

The next morning, when I opened my eyes, Donny was watching me. He was wearing a black Guns and Roses T-shirt and a green gonch.

"Chief," he said, "you got purple eyelids."

It was true. Nobody else had noticed till now, thank God.

"What's your point?" I asked, sitting up.

"My point, dick-smack, is you got purple eyelids and gum in your hair."

I found a lump that tugged at my scalp when I tried to pull it out. "Fuck."

"Classy, man," he said, "real classy."

I heard the clank of dishes in the kitchen. I thought it might be Johnny's mom but it was Johnny. He was wearing the same clothes as last night, and his hair was wet.

"Wanna shower?" he asked.

"Naw," I said. "I gotta go." I stumbled around looking for my jacket.

"Over here," Donny said, pointing. Shit. It was on the floor in the corner.

"You okay?" Donny asked.

"Yeah."

Johnny didn't say anything. I pulled my shoes on. "What time is it?"

"Dunno," Johnny answered.

"You gonna come by today?" Donny asked. "Maybe we could play some cards."

"Don't think so. I got a lot of homework to do."

"Yeah," Johnny added, "and a lot of thinking."

I was up and out the door, sniffing the back of my hands for

76

hash smoke. I needed a shower.

I stood outside, blinded for a minute by the cold red sun. It was windy, and snow was glittering on the grass. The ravens were out and I watched them. They climbed the sky, climbed it to the top. They allowed themselves to be held, to be blown back, let go.

There was the terrible stuck of Bubblicious gum in my hair, the chocolate stain of Jazz's blood on my fist. There was a rash on my face where I had shaved, and the words "I'm a boxer" bounced around my twisted skull.

Jed

SCHOOL DRAGGED ON. My marks dropped, but I didn't tell my mom. She worked hard and didn't need to worry about me. She'd ask, "How's school?" and I'd say, "School's school."

We took a cab when we went to pick up Jed at the airport. I was excited. While we were waiting for him to get off the plane, my mom told me, "I don't know what happened, but Jed's in rough shape."

It was true. Jed was different. I could see it as he walked along the runway to the building. He wore his greasy Husqvarna Chainsaw cap over his salt and pepper hair, but he kept his eyes down. He hadn't been off the plane for five seconds before he lit up a smoke, holding the butt too close to his face. This was crazy. He had quit about three years ago, and it didn't look good on him. When Jed got into the terminal, my mom walked up ahead of me and hugged him. I stood back. Something had changed.

For the first time, I noticed how short he was. He stood about five nine, but I was getting taller. Then I noticed he had cut his hair. He used to be so proud of it streaming down his back. Whatever had happened since he left sure had taken its toll. His gargoyle nose bulbed beneath his slow watery eyes, and he looked tired. He must have felt me watching him 'cause he turned and looked at me.

"Excuse my Slavey, Lare, but I feel like six pounds of shit stuffed into a five-pound bag."

He shook my hand and handed me a big brown bag of dry fish.

"Well, I'm glad to see you, Jed," I beamed.

He nodded. He turned and hugged my mom again. "Verna," he said. "Baby, I missed you."

She hugged him for a long time while I kind of looked away. When they finished, Jed called, "Look at the champ, he's started shaving."

"Take it easy," I blushed. I couldn't wait to have some dry fish.

"*Negha dagondih*," he said.

"*Neghadegondee*," we answered.

In Slavey, in his language, this was how he always greeted us.

"You remembered," he said, and hugged us both for a long, long time.

God Gives Me Little Gifts and These Are Some of Them

JED'S ORANGE SAFETY vest in the closet, Jed's huge green gumboots in the porch, Jed's two rifles in moose-hide sheaths behind the couch, two Buck knives on the counter, one skinning knife on the fridge. Jed's sun-yellow rain gear on a hanger, his two sleeping bags rolled out to dry, his tent in its tiny little bag, his *Birds of North America* and *Plants of North America* books on the table, his moccasins being worn in the house, his binoculars on the bookshelf, big gobs of dry meat in the butter, the smell of the bush in every room in the house. Jed is back! Jed is back! Jed is back!

Itchy Bum! (No Butterflies for Jesus)

"...HERE THAT OLE-TIMER thought it was toilet paper he wiped his ass with, but it was fiberglass!" Jed roared. "You should have seen him on the boat when we were hitting those six-foot waves! Just ouch! ouch! ouch!"

We laughed and shook our heads. We were at the Chinese restaurant, the classiest place in town.

"But boy," he said, wiping his eyes, "no one told us about the killing we'd have to do."

Mom and I stopped laughing and listened.

"You know, after a fire, there's lots of animals that don't make it. They're burned bad and die slow. I lost count of the bears I had to kill, the deer, rabbits, all them animals that suffered. I started to carry a gun with me in the bush just for that. Before, I just used my shovel."

I winced when he said that, and Mom saw. We didn't say anything about it but it was on our minds. My mom sure looked pretty sitting there next to Jed, and I could tell they wanted some time to be alone.

"Hey, little buddy," Jed said, "I noticed that woodpile's pretty low." He eyed my mom. "Hon, you want us to go out and chop six cords?"

"What? The last time you and I went out and tried to cut six cords we ended up setting half the park on fire," I teased.

"How was I to know it was gas in that jerry can?" he said. "I thought it was water. Here I try to put out the little brush fire we got going for tea and the next thing you know I'm hopping around with smoking eyebrows and a bald spot!"

My mom began to laugh, which was surprising. She hadn't been too happy when the park warden had showed up to take our statements and issue Jed a fine. "You guys are a couple of sad Indians."

I studied Jed when he wasn't looking. He had these huge arms he called "the pythons." He sure got his jollies showing them off in shirts with the sleeves hacked off. He was wearing his classic "Denendeh: One Land One People" T-shirt, and it needed a wash.

"Speaking of which, did you start taking drum lessons?" he asked me.

"No," I said. "I don't know any instructors."

"Well, what about the Friendship Centre? Just go and ask. They'll show you."

"Naw, Jed. I don't know. It's not my thing."

"Well, pardner, what about jigging? Didja learn how?"

"No."

"Dja try?"

I shook my head.

"Well, what's it gonna be? The fiddle or the drum? You gotta take a side. It's just like the old-timers say, 'How can you know where you're going, if you don't know where you've been?'"

My mom watched for my response. I remembered my dad taking me in the shed to teach me how to play the drum. I got a chill in the expanding second and scrambled to divert the attention away from me.

"So what happened up in the barrenlands?" I asked.

"Jesus," Jed said, taking a big breath. "Where do I begin? How's my coffee? I ain't tellin' this until I have a full cup."

The woman who had served us was having a smoke in the corner. We tried to wave the other waiter over but he didn't see.

"Hey, Bruce!" Jed yelled. "Hey, Bruce Lee!"

The waiter looked and Jed raised his cup.

We all started giggling. Man, he was fearless.

The waiter came over. "Hey, Jed," he said.

"Howdy, Thomas," Jed said and shook his hand.

"How long you in town for?" the waiter asked.

Both my mom and I looked at Jed for an answer.

"Well," he placed his hand over Mom's, "as long as she'll have me."

Wow!!

Thomas filled our cups. "Dessert?"

"How about some apple pie with ice cream? You want some, Larry?"

"Sure."

"Verna?"

"I'd love some."

"Ice cream?"

"I better not."

"Come on, baby. Winter's coming. You got too skinny without ol' Jed around."

"Oh, all right."

It was so great to see him. I missed him so much. I could feel the weight he was carrying, and it sure was heavy.

"Let's hear this story before we get our pie," I urged.

"Okay," he said, taking a sip of coffee and holding the cup with both hands. "Okay."

Locked in Death

"VERNA, YOU REMEMBER how you told me about that Dogrib woman who drowned her girls?"

"Yes," she nodded.

"Does Larry know the story?"

"No," I said.

"Well." He took a deep breath. "Dogrib woman, I guess. I don't know which community she was from. Her old man took off on her. Said he was going to go on the land and get her some caribou or musk-ox, but he never came back."

Jed took a sip of his coffee and pulled his cap off. He ran his fingers through his hair, put his cap back on, took another sip on his coffee. He flicked a match for his smoke and tried to cover his shaking hands.

"That woman," he continued, "she went crazy waiting for her old man. Her six kids were starving. I guess she got tired of hearing them always asking, When's Daddy coming home? When's Daddy coming home? So one day she lost it. Maybe the devil whispered to her. She took her girls down to the edge of a lake. I guess the water hadn't frozen over yet. She pulled them all into the water and she drowned them. They tried to run away, I guess, but when a woman's crazy, she's strong. She drowned her girls. She drowned them."

Jed did the whole thing again with his hair, cap, coffee and smoke. My mom just nodded.

"Well," he said. "Verna, you wanna know what happened?"

"What?" we both asked.

"I found her husband."

"Where? What was he doing?"

"No," he said, "I found his body when I was on Ranger patrol. Up in the tundra. He was dead. He really did go hunting for musk-ox and caribou, but he died."

"Oh, Jed." Mom covered her mouth.

"He was killed by a musk-ox. I guess he was hunting and he got charged. It got him in the back with its horns, pierced his heart and lungs from behind. Holy shit, he was hit so fast that musk-ox couldn't pull out and they were stuck together. They died together. That man must have bled to death. The musk-ox couldn't eat. They died together. That woman killed her kids for nothing. That man's bones and that musk-ox are still together. I found them."

His voice was shaky, and he took a deep breath. I wondered if he had cried when he first told this story.

"The whole summer was like that, just awful experience after awful experience."

"Jed, man," I whispered. My mom made the sign of the cross.

We were quiet for a bit and Jed looked at us. He was so quiet when he said, "Partners, I'm just glad to see you both."

I looked at my mom. Her eyes were huge. We all took a sip on our coffees.

"Shit," Jed said and ran his fingers through his hair. "Holy shit."

I remembered a song Jed used to sing to me when I had my fire nightmares. There were always flames roaring from room to room. The song was so I could sleep. It went like this:

"How far is heaven?
Let's go tonight
I miss my daddy
and want to hold him tight."

As Cautious as Horses

THAT NIGHT, AS I lay in my bed, I heard Jed talking to my mom. Sure enough, even after a nice supper, they started arguing.

"It's not about you. It's not about me. It's about us," Jed would explain over and over again. "I don't want to lose what we've got."

My mom would say something to him in a calm voice, too low for me to hear. Jed would quiet. I became still, became like death, and prayed to God they'd fuck.

Hello Fogerty, My Old Friend!

I CAME HOME one day and Jed was chopping wood for the wood stove. The days were getting colder and we had had our first couple of snowfalls. Hallowe'en had passed, and surprisingly, the snow hadn't stayed. I put on a pair of Jed's old coveralls, ones he had "forgotten" the last time he left. I loaded up the wheelbarrow while Jed chopped, then I stacked the wood by the porch. After we finished, we took leaks side by side.

"What do you figure there, Jed?"

"I figure," he said, looking down and flexing his ass cheeks, "it couldn't be too much bigger. "

"Seriously." I smiled.

"I figure," he said, shivering from a soothing piss, "you can jiggle, you can dance, but the last two drops always go in your pants!"

I laughed at that one.

"I mean, what do you figure about Simmer?"

"Well," he said, putting his thumb over his right nostril and blowing out a thick gob of snot into the air, "I figure it's not going to be good trapping this year."

"No?" I asked. "How come?"

"When you have lots of snow, the animals follow the trappers' Ski-Doo trails and get caught in the traps. If there's hardly any snow, the animals wander around and don't have to stick to the Ski-Doo tracks."

He put his thumb over his left nostril and blew another gob out onto the frozen ground.

"Can you do that yet?" he asked.

"Naw. Don't want to, either."

"No? They call that a trapper's blow. It's essential if you want to pick up women. They love it."

"Yeah," I answered. "Real classy."

I waited. I think Jed knew what I was getting at.

"Larry," he said, "your mom is the best thing that's ever happened to me. It's just like I've been given a second chance. I don't want to let her go."

"Did you tell her that?"

He looked away. "No."

"Well, maybe you should."

"Yeah," he said. "Mahsi. Hey? You know if my box of tapes is still around?"

Jed had this little cardboard box of tapes, mostly CCR and John Fogerty. Whenever Jed left, Mom would threaten to throw them out, but I always talked her out of it. Sometimes, when I'd come home, she'd be listening to John Fogerty turned low and she'd be crying, missing Jed.

"She hid them downstairs, behind the furnace."

Jed smiled and looked up to the sky. He mouthed a "Thank you, God" and started to do a little jig.

"She couldn't shake old Jed, eh? Boys, that's good to hear."

"Naw," I joked, "she knew you'd come crawling back."

"Time for the pythons to do their magic," he growled.

"Come to papa," I said.

With that we wrestled in the snow. Jed gave me the back-breaker but went easy on me. I gave him a few bannock slaps to the chest but he counteracted them with a souplex and a leg drop. Jed won like always—but this time it took him longer. Johnny had been teaching me the ways of Ninjalics.

Jed and I lay on our backs in the snow, looking up, breathing hard. Our steam rose together to the crystal blue sky.

"Clouds look like dry fish," Jed said.

They did.

"So you got a little trap-line started yet?" he asked.

"Huh?"

"Honeys. Got any queens lined up?"

"Sort of."

"My man," he smiled.

"Jed." I said. "Don't go."

85

He looked at me and winked. "I don't want to, partner. I really don't want to."

Our steam rose together as the snow sparkled on our faces.

Dance

THERE WAS THE annual November dance coming up. Usually I'm a wallflower, but this year I decided I wanted to dance. Clarence Jarome was on stage playing the hits. Everybody was dancing away. Sure enough, all the boys danced the same: left right, left right. But the girls danced just like they did on *Soul Train*. Man, they could really shake it.

I didn't really dance all that hot. One of the few times I had ever danced was with Mister Harris's daughter a year before. She was on her break from private school down south. The song was "Dancing in the Dark" by Bruce Springsteen.

I danced like Jed told me. I closed my eyes and just let the music move me. I started with my feet and got with the beat and then I let the rhythm rise to my hips and then to my chest and even with my eyes closed I wasn't bumping into anyone. I knew I was smiling and it felt so good. Pretty soon I got confident and started spinning around to the song and singing along, and Mister Harris's daughter stopped dancing right when I was dancing deadly. She grabbed me and shook me.

"You can stop the thing with the arms!" she hollered.

She didn't have to go ballistic on me. I just walked the hell out of there and went to bed early.

But this year I decided I was going to have a great time. If you make up your mind about something like that, you'd be surprised at how often it works. I knew Johnny wouldn't show up, and that was just fine with me. Ever since the Floaters, I'd been sticking close to home. Maybe I'd see Juliet. Oh man, what I'd give to...

"Larry!" a voice called out. I looked and I saw her. She cut through the crowd and, boy, she looked good. She was wearing a tight shirt and my favourite black jeans, the ones that hugged her hips and thighs. Man, if she were to fall over right then, I'd hump her leg!

"Hey, handsome!" she said as she crashed into me.

"Hey," I said, composing myself. I could smell the sour sting of booze on her breath and she had a smoke in her hand. She looked kind of rough. Her hair wasn't all that perfect and her eyes looked kind of red.

"Wanna dance?"

"I kinda just got here."

"Oh, come on, Larry. I've been wanting to get you on the dance floor forever."

"Whoah," I said. "Really?"

"Yes, really." She leaned her leg into mine and moved it to the beat. Damn, I wished I was sitting down. My little fireman was getting huge!

"Is there anything wrong?" she asked, and looked at me. She was pretty short, so I could look down her shirt. I could see the accent of her breasts, handfuls, and she saw that I was looking.

"No," I squeaked, "nuthin'."

"Good," she giggled. "I'm glad."

"Where's Johnny?" I tested.

"Mister Hay River?" she said, looking away. "Who cares?"

The music stopped and a slow waltz began. It was Night Ranger's "Sister Christian." "Oh, Larry," she dropped her cigarette and held my hand. "This is my favourite. Come on."

"Okay," I said, not wanting to blow my chance. "Lemme get rid of my coat."

I ran across the foyer and put my coat in the closet. I raced back and Juliet led me to the back of the gym, to where it was dark.

Usually people went there to neck. She wrapped her arms around me and I wrapped mine around her. She pulled me close and ran her fingers through my hair.

"'I won't worry and I won't fret,'" she sang, "'because there ain't no law against it yet.'"

I made a sound but it didn't come out. I closed my eyes and she buried her head in my chest.

"You know," she said and looked up, "there was this guy I knew once. His name was Larry. He was pretty cool, that Larry, but he was real quiet. You could tell a lot went on in that mind of his, but he kept it to himself. And Larry liked to play guitar, except it was always the same note. He would just strum it day after day after day. One day, this angel came down to see him and said, 'Larry, that note of yours is wonderful. We're really happy you like it. But do you think you could spread it out, you know, try a little something new? Like the other musicians?' Larry just looked at the angel and said, 'Those musicians are looking for the right notes. I've already found mine.'"

Oh, if ever I had wanted to melt into liquid and seep into some-body's mouth, it was then. I held her as she undid the buttons on my shirt. I started to look around. Nobody was watching. She started to kiss me and grind herself around my leg. I closed my eyes, and she moved over to my fire-ant nipple. Woo hoo! I could feel her hot tongue; I moved my hands lower. I squeezed her patty-cake ass. I wasn't shy any more. I kissed her hair, then her mouth, and it opened. She lent me her tongue and, somehow, I knew what to do. Yeah, I could taste the booze and nicotine. I wanted more. I ground my body with hers and she hugged me hot.

"Baby," I said, "if you and I lived in a skyscraper, you could hear my love for you six floors up."

"Oh, Larry," she replied, giving me a squeeze, "that's so romantic."

I pulled a tough-guy special and said, "Yeah, baby. Yeah. Let's put the 's' back in sin."

She pulled me down and breathed into my ear, "Let's go."

I buttoned my shirt. She took my hand and we started to leave by the back door. I didn't know where she was taking me, but I was more than happy to go. Shit! I thought, my jacket.

"Juliet," I said. "I have to go get my jacket."

"Hurry up, Larry!"

I sprinted through the gym, saying, "Holy shit, holy shit!" I grabbed my jacket out of the closet and ran through the gym, but I couldn't find Juliet. Oh, the panic! I was just about hollering. Where was she?

Jazz was walking towards me with his arms out. He was wearing his tight little Nike sweat suit, the one that showed off his skinny ass, and he still wore his nose brace. It was white, and his eyes had raccooned black. He looked ridiculous, as if a black butterfly had landed on his face and spread its wings over his eyes.

"Fuckin' foot-licker," I thought. "What a putz."

He strutted up to me, smiling, and I stopped, ready for a fight. People started to surround us like hungry panthers stalking, circling.

"Larry, my man," he said, holding out his hand. "Long time no see."

My mind raced, and I stammered, "Jazz, I'm sorry about your nose. Do you know where Juliet is?" I shook his hand and he applied strong pressure. He was looking into me, and I was puzzled. Were we making up? Where was Juliet? Had she gone?

"I thought she was Johnny's pussy," he said. "I saw her over there," and he pointed to the left. I couldn't see very well because of lights thrown from the sound stage.

"Thanks!" I said, and ran past him. I heard someone call, "Hey, Rocky!"

I turned and I was hit. It felt like somebody took a jackhammer and hit me right in the ear. I saw stars as I went down. I felt something like a boot ram down on my neck. A white flash took me somewhere safe. When I came back, I could see my legs shaking. A million spider-bite stabs shot up my arms and legs, and I was convulsing. I could actually see myself convulsing. I could taste the blood in my mouth where I'd bitten my tongue. I could hear my father shiver again as I brought the hammer down and down and down and, for a second, I could see the stars before they went out. I could see the Blue Monkeys standing with steam coming out their eyes and I went black and heard the hoofs scraping the pavement before he kicked again. I was close to the beast, and he was laughing.

"Now we're even!" Jazz yelled. He was dancing around, holding his arms up. I didn't try to stand. In my head, I could hear Johnny's voice: "Just stay down."

There was a wave of people tackling Jazz. Mongoloid Moose pulled me up. "Juliet?" I thought. "Juliet?" I scanned the couples on the floor, and then I saw her. She was dancing, wrapping her arms around someone else. As I looked, she buried her head in his chest. He had his eyes closed and his mouth open. Johnny! It was Johnny, and he was grabbing her ass, too!

I turned around and saw people pushing Jazz away. He still had his arms raised, and he was laughing. I felt with gentle fingers for any rips in my scalp but couldn't find any. I ran by the track and down the street. I didn't even stop to put on my damn jacket. When I got home, I ran some cold water and looked at my face in the mirror. I'd have my first shiner since the Darcy incident, and my head was pounding. I stood there for the longest time, feeling the throbbing of my skull.

If I could ride the waves of pain, I could remember things. I could feel them. I got a flash of Rae and our house; me standing over him; fire roaring from room to room; me standing in the crowd with a box of matches and the hammer; oh God in Heaven forgive me, my hammer, my secret tusk; me standing over Dad and bringing it down, slamming it down, knowing Dad's passed out, knowing he's dreaming. I wanted to take it away, the sin and dirt and cum and blood in my mouth. I couldn't breathe. My eyes were crying. My lips were split. I wanted to sew stitches through my lips. I thought he wanted me to pray when he said kneel down. I couldn't breathe. I wanted stitches. I thought, Oh God, why is he feeding me mushroom juice? I couldn't breathe. He jammed it so far in I couldn't. I couldn't. I couldn't breathe. I wanted to sew stitches through my lips so he could never fuck me there again. Mother. The flame light. The flame rush. You stand there frozen. Why am I? Why am I—the snow. My face. My skin. It's not supposed to be black.

When I woke up, I was on the bathroom floor, bleeding from my ears. I went into my mom's room but she and Jed weren't there. I made it to my bed and slept for way too long.

I was underwater, but I was coming up for air. I was swimming through Missus Stephenson's legs. She was my nurse, and she did this cheezy exercise with the "pigs" and the lesser burned. We all had to hold our breath and swim through her legs. Except, as I was swimming through, I noticed that she had stumps for legs and that her feet and shins were wooden. I tried to swim faster through her legs, and as I did she began to bleed. There was meat in her blood and I was swimming in it. I tried to rise but I couldn't. I tried to breathe but I couldn't. I tried to scream but I couldn't. When I surfaced, I was in the sniff shack with my cousins. I stunk of gasoline and my father's blood. My hands were sticky. It was in my hair. We were all sniffing and Franky had a nosebleed. He was staggering. There was red paint splashed on his shoes. He was crying. His father was punched out somewhere,

bleeding daddy blood. My cousin Alex was crying, too. His sister
was holding a torn starfish between her legs. And we wept because
we knew we had no one. No one to remember our names, no one
to cry them out, no one to greet us naked in snow, to mourn us in
death, to feel us there, in our sacred place. We wept because we
did not belong to anyone. I cried too for what had to happen. Our
shadows were black. Mine was the only one with fire in its eyes.
I spilled two jerry cans of gasoline empty and there was a lake in
the room. Other kids had paint bags around their faces. Andy's
was leaking blood and propane, so much propane you could push
the air, the water-weight air. And me lighting a hundred sticky
matches, thinking, "The angels are igniting. Their thoughts are
fire-strike matches."

I lit a match. I pushed the air with it and the air pushed back.
And me, the Destroying Angel, screaming, "Let's die! Let's die!
Let's die!!" and my cousin Franky, eyes wide and mouth quiver-
ing, "Larry don't Larry please Larry please—"
then flash
a hot gasoline wind blew through me
then flight
a bath of flames
and the kiss of snow
the flame light
the flame rush
Why am I?
Why am I—
the snow
my back
my skin
rising like dough
splitting into fish scales
it's not supposed to be black

Mother, don't cry. I'm not here. I've buried my bleeding hands in the snow. I don't feel it. I'm far away. Don't pull the blanket off.

Why am I so on fire?

Forever I am in the burn camp. I wear a white mask. The glass in my arms and back begins to work its way out. I learn to talk again. I spend a lot of time inside.

I make a friend. A black janitor. His name is Shamus. He is blind. He says this is not a world for children. He says he can smell three different kinds of snow.

A little girl in the child ward is sick, is scratching herself bloody. We play "bus" and "house." She tells me she is allergic to the sun, but Shamus tells me she is allergic to her own skin. Shamus says what me and my cousins do is called "huffing," says people usually go for the gold or silver paint. That's the stuff that packs the best buzz.

What he doesn't tell me is that murder is a song. A smooth and silent hymn. One I keep inside. For I was raised by butchers.

Shamus calls all the burn victims pigs 'cause they stink and their skin is hanging in strips when they come in. He covers my mirrors and says, "You don't want to see what you've become."

As part of my recovery, they take my mask off and hold a mirror to my face.

"Accept," the nurses say. "You have to accept what happened to you and your cousins."

They make me naked. I see raw hamburger on a human face.

I could hear myself screaming. I would have continued screaming but I opened my eyes, and a Blue Monkey was sitting on my chest, staring into me.

"Hello, Son of Dog," he said, inches from my face. He punched his stump wrist in my mouth, gagging me. I sat up as Jed rushed into the room and threw on the light.

There was blood on the sheets. My head throbbed and my hair

was slick and hot. Jed put his hands through my hair and pulled away, blood on his fingers.

"It's in his ears!" Jed cried to my mother. "Larry! Ohmigod! You're bleeding through your ears!"

My mother stood there, white with shock. I remember holding my hands out to her and seeing her step back, the revulsion in her eyes as I hit blackout.

Hospital

WE TOOK A cab to the hospital. My mom was hysterical, and she made a scene in the waiting room. We had to wait there for a long time. Jed calmed her down and talked to me. "Stay with us, Larry," he said, "stay with us." I kept falling asleep but my mom would slap me awake, worried I could slip into a coma. I was tired. It was about three in the morning.

"Don't let them see my spine, Mom," I mumbled. "Please—"

"Hush," she said, "they won't."

Jed asked, "What's he talking—"

"You," she growled, "never mind."

"Don't learn this, Jed," I thought, "don't ever learn this."

My head fell back. "Jed teddy bear."

I mumbled, "and Mother no mouth."

I looked around. The white towels. The white walls. The hospital. They want to cut off my ears. They say they're burned. They can give me new ones. I am wearing a burn mask to keep the swelling down. "But if you cut off my ears," I said, "what will hold up my glasses?" They look at each other and move away. They don't cut off my ears (and I don't wear glasses).

Jed and Mom kept asking what happened. I told them about Jazz and how he had kicked my ass. Jed wanted me to press charges, but Mom said no. She looked at me. We didn't need the cops. I wasn't bleeding from my ears after all. I had a rip in my scalp.

"Nothing bleeds like a head wound," the doctor said. I got six stitches.

The doctor took some X-rays and gave me a note saying I couldn't eat for ten hours. If I threw up, I was to come back to the hospital where I could stay for the night.

I snapped awake. We were in the hospital hallway. I was in a chair. Across from me, Jed was sleeping, sitting up, leaning against my mom. Mom watched me, and we were quiet. We were so quiet. The doctor had left us alone.

I sat up and reached my hands out. I wanted to take a picture, my mom and Jed looked so beautiful. I softly took Jed's hand and placed it on my mom's. My mom started to cry a bit, really quiet. I then took Mom's hand in mine and watched her right eye. The tear duct my father had destroyed would never work again, so even though she made the sounds of crying, nothing came. For some reason, I thought of Donny, and I started crying, too. Our arms made a perfect triangle.

My mother leaned against me and I could smell her hair. Her face was as hot as mine. My left hand touched my face where my tears ran hot and wet. I held my wet finger to my mother's right cheek and ran a wet trail where her tears should have been. We cried together.

Jed woke up holding both our hands, and we sat there awhile.

"Now now," he said, "now now."

We took a taxi home. When we pulled into the driveway, the kitchen lights were on and someone was standing in the porch. It was Johnny. He came down the stairs and walked towards us. He had his hands in his pockets.

"*A-me-nay?*" my mom asked. "Who's this?"

"Johnny. Can we go inside?"

Jed came close to me and put his arm around me, supporting me so I wouldn't slip. There was ice on our driveway and the stairs were pretty steep. Johnny walked behind us, apart from us. I was hoping he'd try to help me but he didn't.

"Easy," Jed kept saying. "Take 'er slow."

When we got inside, I took my coat off. "Johnny, this is Jed; Jed, this is Johnny. Mom, this is Johnny Beck."

"You're Annette Beck's boy?" my mother inquired. "She was in my English class but she quit."

Johnny blushed.

My mom handed Johnny some blankets from the laundry room. "I have to go to classes in the morning for an exam. Johnny, I want you to wake Larry up every fifteen minutes. Can you do that? Will your mother let you stay the night?"

Johnny went into the kitchen. "I'll just call home."

"You gonna be okay, champ?" Jed asked.

"My ears are ringing."

"I'll get you some rat root," he said.

Jed carried this leather pouch around his neck. He sat down and pulled it out from under his shirt. I sat next to him and watched him take the tiny root out of the pouch. It was like a curved stick, kind of hairy, about the size of a stubby pencil. It was tan-coloured and really thick.

Jed had a little walrus moustache. It was more long whiskers than anything else. He had these black irises that you could see your reflection in if you looked long enough.

"Here, chew on this—but don't swallow it. Chew on it·and let your mouth produce lots of spit. Swallow only after you've chewed it to nothing."

"Okay." I bit off a small chunk, and it stung. The root was sour, bitter. "Hey-a!"

"Yeah, I know," he smiled. "Chew, chew, chew." It was then that I realized his shirt said, "Good-bye Tension! Hello Pension!"

"What is that stuff?" Johnny asked, sitting down across from me, next to my mom.

"Rat root, bitterroot," Jed answered. "Good for stomach or head pains. Good medicine."

"Thanks, Jed," I said. "Mahsi."

"No problem. Who was the kid that did this to you?"

"Jazz. He's a cock."

"John, did you see the fight?" Mom asked.

"No," Johnny said. "I saw Jazz being hauled off but I didn't know it was Lare that he was wasting."

Jed eyed Johnny. "I think that'll be good," he said to me. "The doctor did just about everything he could. We better get to bed. I gotta make your mom some eggs before her test."

"Yeah," I smirked, "Mom and her eggs."

"*Ischa!*" my mom smiled. "Don't you two start."

Jed laughed.

"What's so funny?" Johnny asked.

"Aw, my mom thinks that if you have eggs before a mid-term or a final, you'll ace it. Eggs are supposedly brain food."

"Well," Jed said, "it hasn't failed her so far. Straight A's down the line." Jed flexed his pythons for effect. "Good night, gentlemen."

"Night, Jed," we said together.

"Good night, Larry," my mom said and hugged me softly. At first, I stood there stone man. Then I went limp and gave.

"Uh," I stammered, "good night."

Johnny asked, "You gonna make it?"

"Yeah," I said. I watched my mom walk away. My head was still ringing, but not as much. I felt good, but my mouth was on fire and I needed water.

"That'll teach you not to duck."

"Ha ha," I faked.

"Can I make a sandwich?" he asked.

"Go ahead." I showed him where the meat and lettuce were and I got some glasses out and ran the water. Man, that rat root really stung. I wanted a sandwich too but I wasn't allowed to eat. We took the sandwiches and the water into my room where we could talk. I had a few Iron Maiden flags up. I had the "Trooper" flag where Eddy was running over a hill holding a flag and sword and there were bodies all around. I also had the "Aces High" flag and the "Phantom of the Opera" one. I had a secondhand "World Slavery Tour" poster and a "Somewhere in Time" poster of Eddy where he's half human and half robot. I put the tape on and we listened to "The Loneliness of the Long Distance Runner." I turned it low and the music began.

"I love the artwork on the covers," Johnny said.

"Yeah, Derek Riggs rules."

"Man," Johnny said, "you sure got a lot of tapes."

I had one hundred and four tapes and a few records, but I couldn't play my records any more 'cause we lost the record player to the fire.

I slid into bed and handed Johnny a pillow so he could prop himself against the door. He chewed his sandwich and eyed me. "Jed's neat. He your dad?"

"I hope so," I said.

"You're gonna make it?"

"Yeah," I replied. I wanted to take off my clothes before I fell asleep. I usually slept buck to let my skin breathe. But if I took off my clothes, Johnny might see my scars, and I didn't want that.

"What time is it?" he asked.

"Half past monkey's ass, quarter to your balls."

We snickered.

"Jazz really laid the boots to you."

"I had it coming."

I wanted him to say something about Juliet; I wanted to know how he and she had hooked up. Had he seen us on the floor? Why didn't he help when Jazz was thrashing me?

"Hey, what's this?" Johnny asked, pulling out a certificate that was in between my records. He had finished his sandwich and was checking out my collection.

"'Most loveable boy'?" The certificate was from the children's hospital in Edmonton.

"What happened?" he asked, with genuine alarm in his voice. My certificate was signed by Missus Stephenson and two doctors who helped me out after the explosion. I had it hidden in my *Maiden Japan* record, but it had fallen out. I remembered when they had given it to me; I was being wheeled out in a wheelchair and my mom walked behind us. She had plane tickets to Fort Simmer in her hand, and we left for Simmer right away.

"Come on, Larry," he said. "It says here 'burn ward.'"

"Well," I explained, "I had an accident."

"I guess you had an accident," he whispered. "Burn ward, Jesus."

I was tired and sore. My head was still ringing.

"Was this when Darcy gave you a concussion?"

"No, that was another accident."

"Man, you've had a rough ride. When was this?"

"Before I moved here. Grade seven."

I felt nothing just then. For Johnny or our friendship. It was as if someone had severed the nerves to my feelings. I was only half in my body, and I realized I owed Johnny nothing. He had brought me into the drugs, the circle, the Floaters, and now, I suspected, he had brought me into this.

"Well, what happened to your neck?"

"Whaddaya mean?" I asked defensively.

"Well, sometimes your shirt slips down and I noticed you got some scars on your neck. Come to think of it, they do look like burns. Larry, man, what the hell happened?"

"You wanna know what happened?" I asked with an edge in my voice. "I got kissed by the fuckin' devil, man. They're fuckin' hickeys. He sucked me good."

"Take it easy, Lare," he said, "don't go rank."

I was tense, ready.

"No," I said. "You wanna know where I came from? I just told you. You want to know something else?" I asked. I had nothing to lose. I was tired of keeping it in, and it wanted to be told. It came out like this:

"I had this auntie in Rae. Man, she had it rough. Her old man used to beat her...you know the deal. The thing, though, was that she used to come over drunk and cry cry cry. My mom used to stay up with her and talk. She'd try to get my auntie to leave him, but it was no dice. She kept going back. She used to come over and she'd be drinking. She'd yell, 'Nathan's an asshole. He's a prick!' But she'd always go back. Lots of times, though, if it got too rough, she'd come over and crash. That summer, I was staying out late. My folks didn't mind. They were drinking then. I'd usually crash at my cousins'. Anyways, one night my cousins went into Yellowknife so I went home. I was trying to sneak in but the door was locked. Who the hell locks the door in Rae? No one. Absolutely no one. But someone was up. I could tell. I could see the ghosts on the wall from the tv. So what I did was, instead of knocking, I propped myself up on a log to look in the window 'cause if my auntie was camping over, she'd let me in, and my folks wouldn't know I came home late. I was going to knock on the window, so she would wake up. But instead I seen my dad fucking her."

"What!" Johnny spat. "Holy shit, are you shitting me?"

"Nope. I ain't. He was fucking her and she didn't even know it."

"How—"

"'Cause she was passed out. He was on top of her and he had her shirt up and everything. I wanted to scream. The way she just took it, I could tell she didn't know. My dad fucked her so fast. I couldn't believe it. I ran away..."

"Fuck, man, that's fuckin' fucked!"

"You're telling me?"

He watched me for a bit and we were really quiet. I was shaking as I told the story and tears started to come out. I didn't care. I didn't brush them away. Then they started to come faster. I was crying so hard my legs shook. "My aunt came over the next day and said, 'I feel like someone's been inside me,' but my mom talked her out of it. My mom fuckin' knew!" I cried into my pillow, and in a little while, Johnny reached out and put his hand on my shoulder.

"Holy fuck, Larry," he kept saying, "holy fuck."

He turned the music up so Mom and Jed wouldn't hear me crying.

"Okay, Lare, don't cry, 'kay? Listen, I'm gonna tell you about why I call Darcy 'Thumper.'"

"Just wait," I sniffed. "Fuck, I'm tired of crying."

I blew my nose in my sock and threw the damn sock in the corner. Then I sat up. I was a little happy that I'd finally get to hear this story.

"When I first moved here," he started, "I hooked up with Darcy. He and I used to smoke up, and he hung around Juliet. He hung around all puppy-eyed and he was trying hard to get stinky with her. So one night we went to a party and Juliet was drinking. It's no secret; when she's drinking, she's seventeen going on skanky. Darcy was drinking, too. I guess he had eighteen years of lust and a bottle of Johnny Walker in him, so he starts begging her to make him a man. I heard him asking. She listened 'cause they were buddies and all, and she said, 'Yeah, sure. Why not. You men are all the same.' Darcy had a bone on him a dog couldn't chew! So they go off into a field outside the party. We were at the trailer court. They must have thought I was still partying, but I followed them. I didn't know anyone at the party anyway. So I followed them and watched Darcy spread his coat on the ground. He dropped his pants to his ankles—gonch and all! His fat white ass was waving in the air and she laid down and felt him up. I swear to God he just jumped her like there was no tomorrow and she starts saying, 'I'm not on the pill. Pull out! Pull out!' He must have lasted a whole ten seconds—a real stallion! He pulls out and does his business—really dramatic 'cause she still has her shirt and jacket on and she gets all mad at him.

"She says, 'Aw hell, Darce. How'm I gonna clean that up?'

"Darcy is layin' on top of her and he doesn't give a shit. He's still up in lala land 'cause he got to spunk, and she says—I swear to God—she says, 'You know what I'm gonna call you? I'm gonna call you Thumper 'cause you're so fast.'

"I started to laugh so loud I had to sneak back to the party and pretend I didn't see a damn thing.

"About five minutes later they come back into the party and Darcy's all smily. He looks at me and winks and I ask, 'How was she?' And he says, 'Pretty grand,' and I say, 'Well, whenever you're ready to go there, Thumper!'

"And holy shit, he took a swing at me—you should have seen his face. He was like, 'That name better not stick, man. That better not stick.' That's where we started our warring. The day in the high school was the Monday after. He was passing me in the hallway and I called him Thumper. I shouldn't have, but I did. I couldn't resist. He's an okay guy. He just can't hold his load is all."

Johnny was quiet for a while and I was at the edge of my bed. I pulled my legs up close to my body.

"Jeezus, Johnny," I giggled. "Now that's a story."

"You like that, eh?" He smiled.

My face felt puffy. "I know what you mean," I said, and I went black. I tranced out, and when I came back I was saying, "I really had this thing with the stars. I wanted to be an astronomer. Jed even bought me a telescope and some books. Do you know what the Horse's Head Nebula is?"

"No," Johnny answered. I guess I had been talking to him for a while. He was sitting up, staring straight at me.

"Well, it's a place where stars are born."

"No shit?"

"Naw. No shit. It's on Orion's belt."

"Who?"

"Orion, the hunter. He's got this constellation."

"Like the Big Dipper?"

"Yeah, 'cept it's bigger. One night we're having this meteor shower from the Horse's Head Nebula so I took the pup for a walk—a puppy that belonged to Darcy—but I couldn't see a thing because of the town glare—"

"Wait a minute," Johnny interrupted, "you're not making sense."

I was too tired to stop. "The lights of the town dim the stars. So I took Darcy's pup out along the back roads to where the dog teams are and I could see the stars really clear. The dogs were barking at me but that was okay. The puppy was really scared but I wasn't, and then I seen the meteors flashing as they hit the atmosphere. There was ever lots."

"Lare," Johnny said, "hey, man. You're freaking out."

"Hundreds of them. Yeah, and I started hollering 'cause I could finally breathe 'cause when I wore my mask I could never take a full breath. I was always scared my nose would close up with all the scar tissue. I thought those meteors were angels falling to earth. I was howling with the dogs 'cause the dogs could see them, too. I got so happy and excited I put that puppy down. I started to twirl and twirl and that puppy got too close to one of the huskies. By the time I realized what was happening that puppy was chewed up by the dogs. I mean, they tore her up. That puppy didn't have a chance, and now I have allergies to puppies—"

"Holy shit. What are you talking about?!"

"Yeah, you said it. Holy shit. I was in big trouble. That was Darcy's puppy, and I felt pretty bad. He was on vacation at the West Edmonton Mall. The fuckin' huskies didn't care. Darcy came home a few days later to pick up his pup and I had to tell him what happened. Jed was there in the kitchen in case anything happened. That was the last time Darcy or his mom came over to our house. We've been enemies ever since."

"Larry? Helloooo, Lare, it's me, Johnny. You okay?"

"I was going to spy on the grad bash, you know. I rode out to the golf course to see everyone. I was sneaking up with my bike and I could hear everyone having a good time, whooping it up, and who do I run into on the highway walking back to town 'cause his ride left him 'cause he was being an asshole? Darcy McMannus—you bet. And he's meaner than hell when he gets drinking. I told you what he done to the Merciers. I said hello to him. It was the first time we'd spoken in a while. I thought we could talk or something, but he smoked me and I fell down. I thought he would stop and call it even, but he just kept kicking me with his cowboy boots. He was screaming at the top of his lungs about his dog and how I fucked everything up. I thought people would stop the fight but no one came. I can still hear his cowboy boots scraping against the pavement. I passed out; someone came and found me later on. What did the cops do? Nothing.

I didn't report it. I just told my mom I got rolled by a drunk. I told her it was too dark to see who it was. I had to go to the hospital and everything. Darcy knew I could have reported him but I didn't…As you would say, we were even."

Johnny was sitting up and moving back to the wall. I knew I was scaring him.

"As you would say," I repeated, "we were even."

I enjoyed it. Even though I was trancing, I knew what I was saying. "Yeah, well, I'm tired," I said. "You're not gonna be a dink and wake me up every fifteen minutes, are you?"

"Your mom asked me to."

"Use your best judgment then. I gotta go to sleep. I'm tired."

Johnny's eyes had bugged wide. He pulled his blankets close to him, and I smiled.

I rolled over. "Thanks for talkin'."

For once, Johnny was quiet. I loved it.

"G'night, Johnny," I said softly.

He responded in a lighter voice: "Fuck, I want to go home."

I had a really bad headache, but I was happy inside. The only thing that kept me from roaring with laughter was one question: What do I do about Juliet?

The last thing I heard from Johnny came in a whisper. "Man," he said, "you are fuckin' crazy."

Laundry

IT GOT COLD out, but the days didn't know what to do. It would rain and snow in the same day, only to melt and glitter the next. Some of the dogs in town lay down to pant like lions on the melting snow only to later freeze solid to the ground. They whimpered and whined as their owners tried to pull them free.

You could tell fall was pushing hard and you knew winter was eager too, but just at the last second—the one that determines if it's great sex or an animal act—fall would pull out in a Thumper sort of way and it would all go straight to hell. Winter would be cold towards fall for a bit, but they'd eventually embrace and it would start all over. The days were a tease really, and we all went to bed frustrated.

Juliet still wore her jean jackets and I used the same jacket I had worn forever. Johnny and Donny got new parkas with wolf-trim hoods. Donny said their dad had sent them some cash. Both of them kept saying their dad was coming soon, that he was going to get work up in the diamond mines.

Four of us were standing in the laundry room: Johnny, me, Juliet and Kevin Garner, the slave-day auctioneer. There was a laundry room on each floor in Spruce Manor, and it was a great place to smoke up. We had two joints. The room was pitch black. Kevin was a pusher, and he had hammerhead fingernails. I had spied them when he unscrewed the light bulb so we would become invisible to hallway traffic.

I remembered vaguely that hammerhead fingernails meant tapeworms, so I treated Kevin like a leper. He also had snaggle teeth and greasy black hair. I didn't want to stand next to him but had to, to be close to Juliet. To my right was Johnny. I wasn't really stoned. Every time someone took a puff, I watched Johnny and Juliet in the cherry glare. He had been grabbing her ass all night. I wondered if he had seen us on the dance floor. I wondered if Juliet remembered our tongues, my hands on her ass and the way she had whispered, "Let's go." I knew it had all happened because my shiner was still pretty green where Jazz had cracked me. Johnny told me that Jazz would leave me alone now. We were even.

Johnny and I had put in ten bucks each for a gram of hash, but Kevin had been smoking most of it. In the black, I could hear Johnny's frothy white swollen cow tongue suck and lather up

Juliet's mouth. To me, it sounded as murderous as a wet, bleeding arm stump pulling and popping back into its socket: schluck, schlucka, schluck. The joint came my way. I inhaled the fire and held it without coughing.

I was learning.

I dropped the joint to my right, where Johnny was. It blinked out, and he scrambled for it. While he was down, I grabbed Juliet's ass. She rubbed me back. I smiled. I wanted to lean over and have her right there with Kevin and Johnny in the same room. I stuck my hand down her shirt, and she rubbed me faster. I got to feel her little lace bra!

Johnny said, "I found it," and I backed off.

"What?" Juliet asked, "Who said that?"

"Me...Johnny."

"Oh...," she gulped.

I guess she thought I was Johnny. Haha!

Kevin screwed the light bulb into the socket and the light blared on. Juliet was straightening her shirt and Johnny was trying to suck the joint back to life.

"Turn that light out," Johnny scolded.

"Sorry, boss," Kevin said and unscrewed it again.

"The landlord'll call the cops if he catches us in here."

I was stoned and didn't give a shit about the cops. The room was dark again. The only light came from under the door. I wanted Juliet so bad, but Kevin and Johnny were in the way. I turned my head and looked towards Juliet. I torched the lighter.

"Get fucked, get laid, mony mony!" I said, and everybody laughed.

I aimed the lighter at the joint but at the last second turned and caught the wolf trimming on Johnny's hood. It threw a flashfire trail all around his head. All we saw for an instant was Johnny's mouth in an O. I shoved the lighter into Kevin's hands and pushed him down. We all screamed and stormed out of the room. I was laughing hard as the white smoke bellowed out and Johnny was slapping away at the singed fur. He was screaming at the top of his lungs: "Holy!...you sunova!...I can't believe...!"

I grabbed Juliet and ran into Johnny's apartment. I took her into the bathroom and propped her up on the sink. I kissed her wet and stuck my tongue in her mouth. She was slow in responding so I pulled her close and started dry humping her.

"Whoah, boy!" she said and pushed me back.

I stopped in mid-hump.

"I'm Johnny's," she said.

"What about the dance?" I could hear Johnny's voice out in the hallway still cursing. I backed off and opened the door.

She looked at me and stood up. "What about it? I liked the song. I was lonely."

I walked into the kitchen and slumped down on the counter. I lit up a smoke, breathing deep. Johnny came in all red-faced with his coat in his hands. He kept saying, "Fuckin' black bannock, that fuckin' black bannock!"

I guess Johnny was pretty stoned 'cause I didn't know what he was talking about. He watched Juliet come out of the bathroom, then said, "He gave us our money back, Lare. Here. He says you lit the lighter."

"Kevin's full of shit," I said.

I took the money and stuffed it in my shirt pocket. I grabbed my coat and blew smoke in Juliet's face. She coughed. I slapped Johnny on the back, hard.

"I gotta go. Think I'm gonna listen to Jed for a bit."

"Yeah," he said, running water and putting his hood under it, trying to straighten out the blackened ratty fur. "Later."

I looked at Juliet and said, "Yeah, see ya."

I walked into the hallway, wanting to leave, wanting to get away. I was just about to run down the stairs when I heard Juliet.

"Larry," she called. "Larry, just a minute."

I spun around and held my arms to my sides, ready to spring them out like branches to hold her and carry her away.

"Larry," she said, looking into me. "Listen, I was drunk at the dance."

"Hmmm," I grunted. I pulled the energy out of my arms and braced for the "let's-just-be-friends" speech.

"Larry," she repeated, "I want to tell you something."

I waited. "Yeah?"

"You know about your allergies? You know, to puppies?"

"Yeah."

"Well, I've been thinking. You have to buy a puppy for yourself."

"What?"

"It's all up here." She pointed to her head. "You can get over your allergies. I read about it in this book. I want to be a psychologist."

"Wow," I said. The hurt washed from me and I looked at her. "Thanks, Juliet. Thanks a lot. A psychologist? You'll do it. Good for you."

"Larry," she said, "I'm sorry about the dance."

I pouted. "Well, I'm not."

With that, she held out her hands and ran them through my hair. She brushed my neck softly and closed her eyes. She pulled me close and kissed me on the cheek. I tried to kiss her back but it was crooked, lost. I started to blush and look away. She caught me and looked into my eyes.

"You're sweet, Larry," she whispered. "I know you want to be my secret Santa Claus."

I had an out-of-body experience. She let me go.

"I better get back," she said.

"No," I whispered.

She turned and started to walk back into the apartment. I watched her and I was alive inside. My eyes were watering and my knees were shaking. I half walked, half floated out of the building, heading for the potato field. So I was sweet! Sweet! Sweet! Didja hear that, you fuckin' plague monkeys! Me! Larry! Sweet in the eyes of Juliet. I am the ambassador of love! Woo hoo hoo!

The plastic of my running shoes started to crack from the cold, so I stopped walking. I lit up a smoke and took turns stuffing my free hand in my pocket as I puffed and blew smoke to all the stars. From where I stood, I could see the light from the airport tower slicing the sky every minute or so. I had it all. I had the answer to my allergies, I had the words of Juliet Hope bathing me, straight from her pink, hot mouth—and the northern lights were out, for God's sake! They were green and purple bright. They looked like thick warring wolves running across the sky. I could see Spruce Manor and the high school. Jesus, it had only been three months since I met Johnny. I took another long drag on the cigarette and knew I wasn't the same. I thought of tongues, mothers, snaggle teeth and crimson-red gasoline. I started to shiver.

I flicked the butt when it got to the filter. I turned around and looked at the sky. I could see the rods and cones in my eyes. They were little pin-point haemorrhages. I was so happy I made up a little ditty. It went a little like this:

"Tapeworm, tapeworm

Spin it around

Look up your bum

And see what you've found!"

The moon was getting fuller and from nowhere the thought came to me: "Maybe the moon is God's flashlight."

Jesus Is a Gentle Place and Asses Are for Biting

WHEN I GOT home, Jed was up. He was standing in his gonch with his big belly hanging over. Patsy Cline was wailing, "Sweet dreams of you." Jed's left hand scratched his bum and his right hand offered the phone.

"Partner!" he said. "Phone's for you."

"Thanks," I said. "Nice ass!"

He gave me the fish eye and waddled to bed. Jed had done the dishes—he always did the dishes when he was home—and the kitchen smelled fresh. He told me once the Slavey believed that if you went to bed with a dirty kitchen, your legs would ache when you got old.

"Hello?" I said. I was feeling bubbly.

"Is this Larry? This is Juliet."

"Hey, wow, how's it going, Juliet?"

"Not bad."

Jed always covered the plates and cups with a tea towel as they drip-dried. He told me you had to protect the dishes from spirits. I didn't know about that. It just felt so great to be in my house!

"Not too shabby, hey?"

She sounded kind of sad.

"Is everything all right?" I asked.

"Kind of."

"Where's Johnny?"

"He took off. We kind of had an argument."

"Shit. Was it 'cause I kissed you?"

"No," she laughed. "I didn't tell him about that."

"Good."

"Larry? Johnny told me you were a good storyteller."

I borrowed a classic Jed line and said, "I know a thing or two about a thing or two."

"Well, could you tell me one?" Her voice sounded really distant. I thought maybe she was crying, or had been.

"You're sure you're okay?" I asked.

"Larry, just tell me a story, will you? Johnny said that you were kissed by the devil."

I was quiet. (That fuckin' Johnny)

"Yeah, he said one night you and him were talking, and that's what you said."

I laughed. "I was talking stupid. That was after Jazz used my head as a football."

"Well, it had to have come from somewhere. Could you tell me? Come on, I told you about you having to get a puppy."

"Are you sure you want to hear this story?"

"Yes!"

"First you have to tell me what you're wearing—"

"Larry!"

"Well, just wait," I said. "I gotta ask you something."

"Go ahead."

I was feeling kind of daring due to the impact of her kissing me. "How does it feel knowing you have the best ass in town? I mean, do you lie in bed at night giggling 'cause you got the power? Do you wake up smiling knowing you're breaking hearts with that ass?"

"Larry," she said, "really, when you think about it, what's an ass for?"

Fuck. Talk about crashing. She didn't have to get all grim about it. I started crisis management. I had to save the night. I knew that this was my chance to completely give Juliet something that was mine so much that I would be nothing else. I closed my eyes and decided to let the story lead. I was just the voice, and I knew the story would tell itself. I began:

"Well, one time, long time ago, I guess there was a mother and her son. They were fighting. The boy had seen something and his mother knew what he had seen, but they didn't talk about it. They were arguing and they were both drunk. They began to fight, push, yell and scream. The mother yelled at her boy because he challenged her, but the boy was right in what he had seen and said so. He knew it was wrong. So she banished him. She threw him out. He begged her not to. There was a snowstorm outside, a whiteout, and he had only a jean jacket, runners and a cap on. It was a long way to his cousins', and he said, 'Mom, don't send me out. I'll freeze. I'll die.'

"She said, 'You should have thought about that before you said those things about your father.' The boy was thrown out. He walked by himself. He fell through ice and he died.

"His mother was so sad when her boy died that she sobered up, quit drinking. But she became haunted. She'd see him whenever she was around fire. If someone lit a match or had a fire going, she'd see him, and he'd be freezing, wet. His lips would be blue and she could see his breath. His hair was wet and his jacket clung to him. He was cold and shivering, and he'd be pointing at her from the fire. He'd be saying, 'You...you...you.' And she went mad. She stopped eating, she couldn't sleep and she stopped talking.

"A Medicine Woman in the community noticed the mother was acting strange, so she went to her and asked her straight out what had happened. The woman told her. She said, 'I see my boy in fire. I see him and he's not dead. He wants to die but he's not dead. He's suffering, my boy, and it's my fault.'

"The Medicine Woman said, 'Does your boy have any clothes that he loved?'"

"The mother said, 'Yes, yes! My boy was in cadets last year and he loved his uniform. He was always washing it. Even his boots were always polished.

"'Do you still have it?' the Medicine Woman asked.

"The mother nodded.

"The Medicine Woman asked, 'Why haven't you gotten rid of it?'

"The mother replied, 'It's his. It reminds me of him. It smells like him.'

"The Medicine Woman told her, 'Burn it. You must burn it. You go out someplace and you make a fire. By yourself. You make a fire and you call him. He'll come. You make a fire and you take whatever he says and you say you're sorry. You say you're sorry to your boy and you tell him to sleep, to rest, to die. You call him and he'll come.'

"So the woman did. She made a fire and her boy came. He was like always: wet, freezing. And he was pointing at her, going, 'You…you…you…' And she took it. She took it and she cried and she wailed, 'My boy, I'm sorry. I'm so sorry.' And she offered the clothes to the fire and she burned them. She burned the boots, the uniform, a toque, mitts and long johns. And she told her boy to sleep, to rest, to die, and he did. She never saw him again."

I was quiet, and my blood was pounding in my ears. Juliet was quiet too.

"Larry," she whispered, "that was beautiful."

"No," I said, "that's the truth."

"Oh!" she whispered. "Johnny's buzzing the apartment. I have to go. But thanks for the story, Larry. I'll miss you."

And with that, she hung up.

Jed

I WALKED DOWN to where Mister Ferguson kept his sled dogs and, shit, wouldn't you know it? The snow had covered completely the two hearts I had made the month before! Who knew what had occurred on or within them? And what was the deal with Juliet's "I'll miss you"? I had the last of the dry fish with me and finished it off, running the smoked flesh of white fish over my teeth like cardboard.

"Mmmmm," I said as I chewed.

The huskies weren't there yet as Mister Ferguson kept his dogs in Fort Chip during the summer and fall. The abandoned doghouses sat on both sides of an old Ski-Doo trail in the bush behind my house. When I first moved to Fort Simmer, just after my mom met Jed, he and I would come out here and hunt ptarmigan. It was getting too cold for a jean jacket and a sweater, which is what I had on. Man, my feet were cold in my runners.

Johnny's coat had survived the torch job, but I liked to tease him about it. We both agreed Kevin Garner was prick of the year. I was avoiding my mom these days. I thought she'd know I was stoned. I was also starting to worry about where I was going to keep getting cash for hash. The good news was my mom and Jed were really getting along, not arguing for once. Maybe they were doing it doggy-style! I knew for sure Jed used to smoke up because he had this bullet on the end of his necklace where you could pull the bullet head off the shell casing and there was a roach clip inside. When I first saw it, I thought the roach clip was a pair of tweezers.

I was sitting on a doghouse that had the words "Back in the doghouse again!" painted on the side. There were old slop pails for fish lying around in the cornmeal snow. (That's what Jed called this kind of snow, because it was quite thin and it crunched when we walked on it.) I was just going to light up a smoke I had swiped from my mom when I heard the cracking of twigs and heavy boots on the path. A voice called out, "Zat you, Larry?"

I jumped. "Who's there?"

"Jed. What you're doing?"

"Jed!" I said, surprised to see him. He came into the clearing brushing his kamiks off. "Hey, I was just thinking of you."

"Gretzky," he said. I brushed snow off the plywood roof and he sat down next to me. "That one of your mother's stogies?" he said, offering a light.

"Yeah," I mumbled, "howdjoo know?"

"Export A," he explained, "Verna's brand. Did you save some for Uncle?"

"Any time," I said, taking a puff and handing him the smoke.

"Good man," he said, eyeing me. "There's an acre in heaven reserved for boys like you."

"There better be," I said. "Hey, I thought you quit."

"Did." He took a plug. "Bad year to try."

I noticed that his hands were shaking. "Have a coffee, man," I joked.

He looked at his own hands. "Nervous, Lare, just nervous."

"Scoop?"

"Nuthin'," he lied, looking up at the stars. "You know, I had to cut through the elementary playground today. Kids in elementary are already starting to chew snuff."

"Yeah, it's pretty bad."

"Hmmm," he said, scratching his scruff.

"You gonna pass that smoke back over here," I asked, "Uncle?"

"What? Oh…hey, look at you, a young man sticking up for himself. Yeah, sure, here you go."

"Thanks."

"Been smoking long?" he asked.

"Naw, just started."

"Then you stain easy, I guess."

"What?"

Jed held up his pointer and middle fingers and pointed to the top digits. He motioned for me to look at mine. I did. They were stained yellow; same with my fingernails.

"Jesus, Jed, what am I gonna do? Mom's gonna kill me."

"Verna knows."

"What?"

"Larry, your mom knows a lot of things you think she doesn't."

"I guess."

"And me too," he said. I met his eyes.

"If you ever need to talk," he continued, "you just ask and we'll come down here."

"Okay," I said. "Thanks, Jed."

And we were silent.

"Listen, uh…Larry, your mom is trying to get me to take you out on the land again."

"What? The last time we tried, we didn't get any moose. And when you had that bear in your sights, the gun didn't go off."

"Dud," he explained. "It was a dud. And those moose were Ninjas. We can go somewhere else."

"Where?"

"Tsu Lake. Renewable Resources takes their first-year students out to bush camp for a month, and they'll need someone to cook or teach fire science. I talked to the head instructor today and it looks like a go."

"When?"

"March, winter camp, and I could stick around until September for their summer camp."

"Oh yeah?" I asked. "Thinking of sticking around?"

"Well," he said, looking at his shoes and taking a deep breath, "I think I'm going to try to stick around more than I have been."

(Woo hoo! Right fuckin' on!) "Cool," I said.

"Yeah. Your mom and I are gonna give it a go—" Then he

said really quick, "Boy, it's getting cold out here. You come out here often?"

"Yeah," I said, "when I need to think."

"Anything particular?"

"Naw. I'm happy for you and Mom, though."

"Yeah, well. You gonna stick it out here or are you going to come back to the house? I could gab on and on, but I feel like some hot chocolate. You want some?"

"Sure," I said. I hadn't had hot chocolate in ages.

"Let's play some cards, see if I can win some money back. Hey, you see that snow on the trees over there? You know what a Cree woman once told me? She said that when the snow is on the trees like that, it's the breath of the caribou, they are so close."

"Wow."

We got up, and I brushed my pants off. We walked up the trail together, talking and laughing.

"Oh yeah, Larry," Jed said, "about your friend...John?"

"Yeah?"

"You know when you got into that scrap, and afterwards I asked him if he had seen you in the scrap?"

"Yeah?"

"Well, Larry," he said, stopping and putting his hand on my shoulder, "that boy was lying to us when he said no."

"How do you know?" I asked defensively.

"My spider senses were tingling the second I met him."

We walked home together, crunching snow beneath our heels. Something suddenly hit me.

"Jed? 'Member the Dogrib story you told me? The one about how we came to be?"

"Yeah."

"'Member those kids that made it back to the bag?"

"The ones that turned back to pups?"

"Yeah. What did the mother do with them?"

"I didn't tell you?"

"I don't think so. I can't remember."

"She killed them, Larry."

Phone Call Yippety-Skip!

AS I WAITED for Juliet to pick up her phone, I said her name out loud to myself. I rolled it around in my mouth, savouring each syllable as if it were a sweet and delicate Christmas.

"Juu-leee-et," I whispered, "Juu-leee-et."

I had rewound the Outfield's song "Baby, When You Talk to Me" and got it ready so that when she answered, I would press "play" and she'd hear it. Man, she just had to know how I felt. I also had Judas Priest on standby: "Turbo Lover" was set to go, and if the conversation followed along, I had backup, too. Van Halen was locked, cocked and ready to rock.

The phone line rang again and a woman picked up. "Hello?"

It was Missus Hope. I took my finger off "play."

"Good evening," I said, "is Juliet in this evening?"

"Why?"

"...Um, I'd like to talk to her," I answered.

"She's grounded." CLICK!!

Grounded? I held the receiver. What the hell had just happened? Maybe Juliet was getting heck for something. Or maybe her mom had recognized my voice as one of the losers from the night I smoked up. Yeah, that had to be it.

"Man oh man," I whispered, "the shit I take."

I went downstairs and lit the wood stove. Mom and Jed were out partying it up because Mom had done really well on one of her exams and it was a full moon. They always celebrated the full moon, every month. In summer, we'd have a back-yard party and Jed would cook—that is, if he was in town. I sat down in the dark. Why was Juliet grounded?

Just then, I heard the neppp-neppp-neppp of a three-wheeler pulling up in my driveway. I could hear the gravel roar as someone skidded to a halt, and the clunk-clunk-clunk of boots as someone flew up my stairs. There was the ding-dong of the doorbell. I turned on the outside light and holy shit—it was Darcy McMannus! Maybe he was here to kick my ass and give me another concussion. I opened the door, just a little bit.

"Hey, Darce," I said, "how's it going?" I kept my distance and got ready to duck.

"Hello, Larry." He had his helmet and gloves in his hands and he was looking down the street, not making eye contact. I took a look at his nose and got ready in case I had to deck him one.

The circle, I thought, the circle. I was scared shitless.

"Your old lady's out, huh?" he asked shyly. "Can we talk?"

"Yeah," I said. He looked pretty sad, so I took a chance. "Come on in. Put your helmet over there."

"It's getting colder," he said. "Ski-Doos will be out soon."

"Yeah. You still got that Phazer?"

"Naw, rolled it. Sent her out to Hay River to get fixed but I can't pay for it."

"That's the shits."

I could tell he had something to say, so I motioned for him to come sit down.

"Heard about you and Jazz busting each other up."

"It was stupid," I said.

"We got trouble."

"How?"

"Ahh, shit," he said. I thought he wanted to fight. "Juliet's gonna have a kid."

"What!?"

"She called me up crying. She's fuckin' preggo."

"No way!"

"Yeah."

"Are you fuckin' serious?"

"Do I look fuckin' serious?" He glared, and I realized he was scared. "Shit, man, the whole town knows."

"How?"

"Nurses, doctors, fuckin' everyone in this fuckin' town!"

"Oh man, oh shit," I said. There was panic in my voice. I sat down. I stood up. I looked in the mirror. I ran my fingers through my hair.

"She's going to Edmonton tomorrow, gonna stay with her aunt," Darcy said.

"Is she going to have it?"

"She says she wants a fuckin' kid," he said. "I don't know. Fuck. She wants to see you before she goes."

"Me? What?" My mind was racing. What the fuck was going on?

"Yeah, why you?" he asked suspiciously.

"Where is she?"

"You gonna speak to Johnny fuckhead, too?" he asked.

"What does she wanna do?"

"You wanna double-bank Johnny?"

"What?"

"We could go over there and roll him."

"No. Does Johnny know?"

"Hell yes! And he hung up on her, the cock. He won't speak to her."

I put on my shoes and jacket and Darcy ran outside and started his machine. I got on the back and we motored down the back streets of town. It was snowing out, and I started to get jittery on the back of the bike. I realized this might be the last night

Juliet would ever be in town. I couldn't believe it. We wove past the church, past the drugstore, through the baseball field, past the Pair-a-Dice motel, under the water tower, past the graveyard and into the park behind her house.

In the park, we scared two ptarmigans that were sleeping in the snow. Their white wings flicked to their sides and they flickered ahead of us, like calm white hands. One flanked right, but the other smashed into our windshield.

Darcy jumped off his trike, ran over to it and knelt down.

"Shit," he said. "Fuck!"

I walked over and stood looking at the destroyed bird. It was as big as a baby pup. It was pure white except for its beak and eyes, which were jet black. It was suffering, trying to move. Blood came from its mouth, and it tried to talk to us, moving its beak.

"Look at that," Darcy said.

I picked up the warm bird and held it to my chest. With my left hand I held its back and with my right hand I twisted its neck, snapping it.

"You're fuckin' mental?" Darcy asked and stepped back.

I handed him the twitching bird. "Her room, which one is it?" He looked down for a bit. "See the blue light in the basement?"

"I could be a while."

He was quiet. I didn't want him hanging around.

I laughed. "I'm serious, I could be a while."

"Don't matter," he said, petting the ptarmigan. "I'll wait."

I hopped the fence and crouched low. I peeked into the room through the curtains.

Juliet peeked back, wiped her eyes and waved me in. I motioned "How?" and she opened the window.

"Climb in," she whispered. "Quietly."

I did. I scraped my back and belly, but I did it. She guided me through, saying, "Shhhh, shhhhh."

When I landed on her bed I lay there, and she looked at me with those eyes. The room was completely blue from the light thrown off the TV. It was tuned to the blue channel, the one with the local community announcements about birthdays and bingos.

"Is it true...about...?"

"Yes," she said. "I leave tomorrow."

"What about Johnny?"

"He's moving to Yellowknife."

"Isn't he going to—"

"Shut up about Johnny."

Her room was simple: just a bed, a TV, books, a hope chest and Japanese fans all over the walls and ceilings. There were hundreds of them, small and large. They looked like moths in various states of flight.

"Juliet—" I said.

She kissed me.

"But what about your—?"

"I want this baby, Larry. Babies are perfect."

She pulled my shirt over my head and let it fall to the floor. I stood there, cold, and I started to shiver.

She said two words: "One night." She looked at me and I felt it. I felt alive, like I had fallen from the sky with the grace of God, with the petals of God, and I had finally spread my wings.

"Don't you want to crawl into this shirt with me?" she asked. I was hypnotized.

She stood there, and I swallowed her image. It burned my eyes and mind, scorching them pink, and I became a disarray of limbs as I tore the rest of my clothes off. I grabbed her and kissed she kissed back and I blew shhhhh grabbing her ass and she pushed me away and threw me down pulled the covers up and over us pulled her pants and panties off pulled me close. I became gentle beneath her. I stuck my tongue in her ear and we began. We got so loud and I got so hard I thought I'd pop. I understood now the quick gush of Darcy. I was on fire with a silk black fox tasting my fingers.

"I don't want your hand inside me," she said and moved closer. "Come on, Larry."

I rolled on top of her and her hand placed me there. She was soft giving flesh that I took with my tusk and she was hotter than the centre of the sun, like a long never-ending swallow. I couldn't go deep enough. She shivered inside and bucked under me and I was buried in her hair. She was in my mouth in my throat and she raised her ass under me and (call her snowbird) our meat baby-blush pink (call her raven) the monkeys slept and I swam under her shirt and grabbed her breasts, one of which had slid from under her bra and I filled my mouth with her a warm dove I filled my throat with her and she was in my lungs and my tongue little lightning strikes against her nipples she threw me over and I fell out of her. We gathered it together and I was not alone; I was not forgotten; she established territory by riding position and teeth, hot little teeth against my throat. She scratched my back and I almost felt it. One hand was up her shirt, the other squeezed her ass her mouth was open her eyes were closed I watched what I did to her and I loved it. We went for spice and my tusk pulsed inside her my heart was inside her and it was sweet violation and she pulled me tight and this was the place of Jesus this was the place of Jesus this was the place of Jesus. I was touching her soul and I began to drown. There was no shame in being loud and crying out as Juliet pumped harder and moved like flames like blades of wicked fire, her tiny toes sliced my legs, her razor nails scratched my back and she felt the scales.

"Look at me," I said. "Look into me, just look at me."

She did

and I wasn't alone

I wasn't forgotten
I wasn't dead
There was no small town
There was no killing
I wasn't bad I was clean
I arched so hard I thought I'd touch the back of my skull with my feet. It was like a bullet passed through me. I sank deep within myself where I was untouchable, where I was awake but sleeping. I fell so deep I was in my fingers, the filaments of my hair, and Juliet was far away pumping me, far away melting me, and I panted and lay there spent like winter coming, like fall dying.

As I sank back, she was hugging me, panting, "Holy shit, holy shit." And I was selfish. I lay there and breathed

breathed

breathed.

She hugged me as we lay on our sides. I felt so good. So clean. She ran her fingers against me. She blew herself into my ear.

"Your back," she kept saying. "Larry, what happened to your back?"

"Shh," I said, "come on now."

"Were you burned?"

"You'll never believe me."

"Come on. It's like running your hands over a jigsaw puzzle."

I was quiet. I looked at her neck. I felt her breasts against my chest. They were warm, skinned doves.

"Do you think," I said, "that when a Russian man is inside a Russian woman, they both feel like we just did?"

"What?" she said.

"Well, it felt so good to be inside you," I said, "so hot and spicy. It must feel like that for every man who's ever been inside a woman. I bet it feels the same."

"Thanks a lot," she said and tried rolling away.

"No, Juliet. Please. I just feel so happy. This was a dream come true for me."

"Yeah, well, tell me what happened to your back and we'll call it even."

I thought about it for a long time. I wanted to get it perfect. "I was sewn into the belly of an animal."

She was quiet and I waited for something. She started to giggle.

"God, you are so weird," she said. I ran her hair through my fingers and thought of the fireweed in the ditches in spring, how good it smelled, how the colour ran off like blood on your fingers.

"I love you, Juliet," I said and I fell asleep.

Where the Blue Light Falls

WHEN I AWOKE, she was crying. I sat up.

"I'm scared," she said, and hugged me.

"Juliet, what are you going to do?"

"Go to Edmonton."

"What about us?"

"Larry, I wanted to do this."

"With me? You never even look at me."

"Larry," she sniffed, "just because I'm not looking at you doesn't mean I'm not watching you."

I was quiet. I held her. I looked at her. I kissed her face. She looked down. I kissed her eyelids closed.

She put her hand between us and over her tummy.

"I have to tell you something," I said. "I'm not going to lie. I have to tell you. I have this God-shaped hole in my heart, and I think you do, too."

She started to cry hard, and I could feel her hot tears fall down my chest.

"Juliet," I whispered, "I have to ask you. Why did you use crutches in grade eight?"

She was quiet for a bit, thinking. "Did you believe what they said—that I had the dose?"

"I didn't." It had just hit me we hadn't used a condom. (Shit!) "But I heard what they said."

"Larry, don't you get it? Every high school needs a whore: Yellowknife, Hay River, Fort Smith. I'm Simmer's."

"I don't think you're a whore," I said. "I think you're beautiful."

I kissed her nose, her cheeks, her forehead. I kissed everything I could reach. My hands held her ass and I squeezed.

"I'll tell you what really happened," she said, "but you can't tell anyone. Promise?"

We shook. I wouldn't let her hand go. "Promise."

"That was probably the best summer of my life," she began. "I had it all. I was going to a lot of fun parties then. The seniors really knew how to rock. They'd party at the racetrack, the golf course, the towers. We could go for days. There was this guy from Yellowknife. A real babe. His name was Jungle, and he was a dealer. He had this car he wouldn't let anyone drive. And this car was deadly. Class. I knew he had his eye on me, and he let me take his car out to the dump. I had it up to a hundred and twenty klicks an hour on the highway. I remember hearing those four barrels open up. We were flying, Larry, flying."

I nodded and held her close. God, she was beautiful. I kissed her and she looked away. She kept talking.

"One night we were partying at Kevin's trailer. I needed a place to pass out. I couldn't go home. So I went to bed in Kevin's room and told Kevin to watch out for me. I passed out in that room awhile. When I woke up, I knew someone was lying behind me. I pretended to sleep. I was awake, but I kept my eyes closed. It was a man, I knew. The bed was shaking. I turned around and it was Jungle. He was jacking off, watching me. I started laughing. He looked so stupid. I don't know why I laughed like that. I'd never seen anyone do that before. The next thing I knew, he had me by my hair and he flipped me onto the floor. I landed on my leg and we both heard something pop. I started screaming and he grabbed my throat. No one was there, anyway. They'd all gone for more booze. Jungle shook me and said if I ever told anyone about what I'd seen, he'd kill me. He said he knew someone in Yellowknife who killed people and that all it took was two thousand dollars."

"Holy shit." I sat up. "What a fuckin' idiot."

"So that's why I had to use crutches."

"What happened to Jungle? Did someone kick the shit out of him?"

She shook her head. "He got in his big beautiful car and took off."

We were quiet.

"The sad thing is," she said, "I would have let him."

"No," I said, "no."

"I can still hear those four barrels opening up," she said. "We were so free on the highway, Larry. You should have seen us. I couldn't stop laughing."

I let out my breath. Juliet ran her fingers through my hair and we kissed for a while. She held me for a bit, and then firmly said, "Go."

"Wait," I said.

"Go! I mean it. I have to leave soon."

I got up. The furnace came on in the house and I felt the hot air from the vent above wash over me. I stood up, naked, free. I grabbed my clothes and looked at her. Her eyes went wide when she saw my scars but she said nothing. She got up off the bed. "Good-bye, Larry. Thank you for a wonderful night."

I waited. She left the room. I heard the shower start up and still I waited. I wanted her to come back so we could talk and kiss. I looked at the Japanese fans, and it hit me: all the wings were clipped.

I knew she wasn't coming back. I tried to fix the bed, but I knew she wanted me to leave. It was a moment. And I knew it was gone. I saw her hairbrush on a little table she had. It was surrounded by pink candles, a gold chain coiled around them. I picked up the brush and pulled out the longest hair I could find. I wrapped it around my finger. I kissed it. I put it between her mattress and the box spring. This way, when she died, she'd have to come back, find this one hair, remember me, remember us, remember what happened before flying back to heaven. I climbed out the window and into the snow. I could taste her kisses in my mouth and I was hollow inside. I had monkey hair, and the snow was coming down. I took a big breath and filled my lungs. I followed my fading footprints back to where Darcy had dropped me off. He wasn't there.

In the snow, I saw the twisted lump of the ptarmigan. I picked it up. It was frozen thick and solid.

"Fuck," I said. I held it close to my chest, its black glass eyes open, staring at me through snow.

"Rest," I said, "rest and sleep."

As I started to walk, I heard Darcy's three-wheeler nepp-nepping down the road. I ran onto the street and waved him down. My heart stopped. I could see he had a passenger.

"Shit!" I thought, "he's got Johnny!"

I thought they'd jump off and hang a lickin' on me, but the engine died and all was quiet.

"Here it comes," I said to myself and advanced.

"Hey, Cheemo!" called Jazz's voice. "How's it going, Dogrib?"

I didn't answer but walked straight up to him. Darcy, pulling his helmet off, said, "Cool it."

I looked at Jazz and let him know I was ready to rock again. He glared back and smiled.

"As if…" he said.

"Fuck you," I said. "I'm your fuckin' dad."

His eyes went wide.

"Talk to her?" Darcy said.

"Yeah."

"She still wants to keep it?"

"I guess."

"Well, Johnny tub-of-shit ain't going nowhere for a while," Jazz said. "We got him good. Didn't we, Darce?"

"Yeah," Darcy said, "we got him."

The motor started again and Darcy put on his helmet.

"Check out the smile on Dogrib's face," Jazz said. They took off, snaking down the road.

I walked past the Pinebough and down Main Street. The snow started to fall so thick I could pet it on its way down. There weren't any cars on the streets, and I did a little jig at the four-way intersection.

"Fuckinrights! Fuckinrights! Fuckinrights!" I giggled, twirled and ran through the potato field. I knew I should feel bad, but I was holding a little piece of heaven in my heart.

"This one's for Juliet! Thank you, God! Mahsi cho!"

I was still carrying the ptarmigan. I stuffed it in my jacket.

As I headed home, I saw a truck backed right up to Spruce Manor. The lights and windshield washers were on and the engine was running. Clothes were flying out one of the building windows and landing on the new snow.

I slowed down and started to watch, and I saw Johnny trying to catch the clothes as they landed. I heard a woman's voice yelling, "Come back! Come back! Come back!" and I could see Donny being pulled out of the building by a tall skinny man. Donny was in his jeans and T-shirt, calling, "Johnny, we gotta go! Dad says we gotta go!"

I ran past the truck and got close to Johnny. He turned like he was expecting to be hit. He had a black eye, and blood crusted around his nose.

"Fuck!" he yelled.

"The hell's going on?"

The clothes kept flying out the window, and the woman's voice was crying, "That'll teach you. That will teach you!"

I helped him gather up his cold clothes.

"Fuckin' Mom's having a conniption. Dad's here to pick us up."

"You going back? To Hay River?" (Big Kahoona)

"Going to Yellowknife."

"Johnny!" a voice boomed. "Get in the damn truck!"

"Coming," he called weakly.

"What about Juliet?" I asked.

He looked at me and covered his face.

"Johnny," I said. "What about Juliet?"

"Jonathan Beck," his father hollered, "get in the truck!"

"You stupid kid!" the woman called.

Johnny looked straight at me and said, "She fucks good, don't she?" He smiled. "It could be your kid now."

I went to push him down but he caught my arms and pulled me towards him, right into the crook of his elbow. I went down. Before I could react, he sat on top of me, landing full velocity on my chest, knocking the air out of me. I huffed as all my ribs crushed. I tried to bring my thumbs up towards his eyes and throat but he put his heavy legs on me. I heard the slam of the truck door and I heard someone running towards us in the cornmeal snow. The ptarmigan in my jacket felt suddenly warm as Johnny pulled his fist back behind his skull. I heard his dad scream, "Leave him alone! We gotta go!"

Johnny was going to bring that war hammer down and bust my nose. I knew it; he knew it. He was going to bring me to where I brought Jazz. But he couldn't. He didn't. He just stayed like that and looked at me.

"I'm just a kid, Lare," he whispered. "I want to be beautiful just a little bit longer."

His father dove straight into him. They started to wrestle in the snow, with his father yelling, "Fuck sakes. Let's go!"

Johnny cried back, "Fuck off! Let go!"

I stayed there on the ground, looking at the night as they screamed at each other. My back was cold. The northern lights were washing the sky with green and blue hands. I just lay there and felt fucked.

Surprisingly, Donny walked above me. He was chewing on a carrot.

"Hey, chief," he said, looking down, oblivious to the fighting, "Johnny kicked your ass, huh?"

I nodded.

"Hey," he said. "You gonna remember me tomorrow?"

I nodded. I was still out of breath.

He smiled. "You gonna remember me in two weeks?"

I nodded and felt my ribs.

He started to laugh. "You gonna remember me in three months?"

"Yeah," I said.

"Knock knock."

"Who's there?"

He kicked snow in my face. "Forgot me already, chief."

He walked off. I tried to sit up and spit the snow out of my mouth. I watched as Johnny was hauled off by his father. He was crying, trying to get away. His father opened the door and threw him in, then strutted over to the driver's side and slammed the door. I saw Johnny rise for a moment and try to raise his hand in a good-bye. Donny stood up and yelled, "We're off to Yellow-knife! Sol later, chief!" The truck threw snow as it sped off down the road.

I stood for a minute and watched the truck disappear onto the highway turnoff.

"Sol," I called softly after them.

I listened, and I could hear Johnny's mom crying from the open window.

"Fuckin' kids," she kept crying. "You fuckin' kids."

The dead ptarmigan had fallen out of my jacket. I picked it up and headed for where Old Man Ferguson kept his dogs.

Me

AND WITH MY hands, I buried the beautiful white bird as best I could. In the clearing ground where I had created the two hearts, I dug and dug until I hit the frozen earth. I placed the ptarmigan in the snow and covered her.

I said, "Rest."

I said, "Sleep."

I said, "Die."

And I wept because I knew I had someone

someone to remember my name

someone to cry out my name

someone to greet me naked in snow

someone to mourn me in death

to feel me there

in my sacred place
and I wept because I did not belong to anyone
I was not owned
not with mate
but I smiled too knowing this because I knew my life was
    still unwrapped
I would in time
find one to call my own
mine to disappear in
to be...

Short Stories

Where Are You Tonight?

JULIET HOPE IS alone and lonely and the moon is the light of ache and if-only. *I want a baby. I want a baby. I want a baby. Even with my eyes closed I want one. To be full. To never be alone again. To raise and hold. To be one with someone. The world will leave me alone then. And it can be just us. We can play all day and I can watch you grow. It will be just us and I'll never have to share my love with anyone else again. With babies, you can start over, and I already love you,* she thinks. *I already do.* She thinks of Darcy. *That was a mistake. One day out of my life. One time and I've got him if I need him. There's Larry, the puppy dog. Always watching me. Always wondering, I am sure, what I'd be like. And then there's the new boy: Johnny. God, he's gorgeous. He's beautiful. That face. Those eyes. Those hands. He's kind. I can tell. A girl knows. He's almost the one.*

Why have I never had a girlfriend? she wonders. *Oh. I know. It's because I'm a threat. Always have been. Even when I was little, I could tell women hated me. How their husbands watched me grow. How the principal and gym teacher and Mr. Harris watch me now.*

She touches her tummy, sweeps her hands slowly over herself. *Soon, my baby. Soon.*

JUNIOR RACES HOME from pumping gas at Norm's, the only gas station in Fort Simmer. *This is it*, he thinks. *This is it!* For the past two months, someone's been playing with his stereo and cranking his tunes. He knows it's Karen. Just knows it. He's hidden his speaker cables in his room but they're never put back the way he'd left them. He's given his sister heck, but she denies, denies, denies. "You're gonna blow my speakers!" he yells at her, but she swears it isn't her. Junior's been making money on the side at the teen dances as a DJ. Two hundred bucks cash on the dash every

Friday and he knows what packs the dance floor. He's got a system: Hip Hop, Dance, Techno, Country—repeat—

He races home an hour earlier than he told his family he'd be because tonight's the night: he's going to catch her doing this. She's been spending too much time at home now that she got barred from the Pinebough. Halfway up Ptarmigan, he kills the lights on his truck and coasts two houses down. He slams it in park and gets out, starts running. Sure enough, he can hear the house shaking with the bass! Karen's cranking the tunes so much the house is booming and bumping. *She's gonna blow my speakers!*

Junior picks up the pace. He can't place the song, but it's drum thunder and brutally loud. *This is it!* he thinks. This is finally it. I'm gonna catch her and she's gonna get it! But what is that song?

He races into his house and opens the door with a "Jeezus, Karen!" when he catches his dad, Reggie, dancing with his shirt off. Reggie is in his blue long johns and dancing up a storm, hopping up and down with his eyes closed, his arms twirling, and it's not a song Junior owns. It's his dad's music. It's Hand games music.

Whoe whoe whoe whoe whoe whoe
yah yah yah yah
whoe whoe whoe whoe whoe
yah yah yah yah…

His dad's supposed to be hunting but he's home. Junior freezes and sees his dad hopping around to the Hand games music. He can hear the hypnotic drumming of twelve men hammering twelve caribou drums all singing in this rhythm that staggers Junior's breathing because it's so powerful and loaded with medicine. His blood roars and his eyes cross with the feelings he gets when he watches his dad play Hand games.

Reggie has this move where he flutters his hands like ptarmigan wings in front of the opposing team as he makes a "hass" sound to confuse them, and he's doing it now: "Hass, hass, hass."

The drums boom over and over. He can hear the spruce drum sticks pound the skins and his dad, topless and free, is singing along, eyes closed, wiggling his hips, hopping up and down with his big grown arms up like Hulk Hogan after a body slam. *Man*, Junior thinks as he switches from outrage to shock. *Dad can really move.*

When he first started to play last year, he looked like a big baby wearing water wings hopping up and down in a Jolly Jumper. As soon as Junior thinks that, his dad opens his eyes, drops his arms and covers his nipples, his little belly, back and forth, back and forth.

"Dad?" Junior mouths.

The drumming and singing are still blaring. It's a live recording and Junior can hear people whoop it up as they watch the drum competition. His dad has a little moustache now and the shadow of a goatee. His hair has grown and his cheeks are burnt from the wind.

Junior looks down out of respect and doesn't know if he should leave or what. His dad scrambles out of the kitchen and races into Mom's sewing room. Junior stands there and closes his eyes. *What did I just see?* He tries to find lyrics to the chanting and singing but it's that "Whoe whoe whoe whoe whoe whoe yah yah yah yah whoe whoe whoe whoe whoe yah yah yah yah..." times a hundred.

Junior has never seen his dad dance and he marvels at what a strong body his dad has. It's been forever since they shared anything. His dad's been hard on him this past year: more chores, more expectations, more demands. *And here he is: Dad's the one! I've gone after Karen all this time for cranking my tunes, but it's been Dad?*

Reggie comes out of the sewing room with his favourite red

AC/DC T-shirt on, blushing and laughing, before going into Junior's room to kill the tunes.

Junior stands there in the porch and sees his dad out of breath and embarrassed. He's actually blushing when he says, "Uh, hi." He starts laughing again and claps his hands once—as if to clear the air.

"I thought you were hunting," Junior says.

"I was, but we got called home. Our team made it to the Dene Hand games Competition in Rae."

"Wow."

"You should come with me," his dad says. "I could teach you." He's trying to be serious but bursts out laughing again and Junior can see that his dad's ears are purple. It's been years since his dad has laughed out of embarrassment and Junior starts laughing with him. He starts laughing so hard and can see his dad walking towards him. His dad's still wearing his blue long johns and a gonch underneath, thank God. His dad hugs him and they laugh together. "That's your grandfather's song," his dad says and Junior holds his father, feels his whiskers against him. "Come with me." His dad smells of smoke and the land. *He's smoking again*, Junior thinks. *I won't tell Mom*. He closes his eyes and grabs his dad with a hug and a wish and a *Thank you, God, for this*.

"Okay," he says to his father and he can still hear that song: the song of his grandfather.

KEVIN GARNER IS trying to listen to his Granny as she spreads her Bingo sheets out. She's talking. More stories. Half English. Half Dogrib. She's got two Bingo dabbers ready to go and her lucky statue of the Virgin Mary that glows in the dark. As a kid, he used to watch the statue when he'd sleep on the couch, and he was convinced it levitated towards him ever so slowly throughout the night. It used to scare him so much that he'd half pray and half blubber to her, "Let me live, Virgin Mary! Let me live. Do it for Jesus. Please. My Granny needs me. She needs me. Who'll take care of her if I die young? Plus you're a virgin and holy. Don't be cheap and kill me. If you kill me you're cheap, okay?"

As much as his Granny loved the church, Kevin never trusted it. He still didn't understand The Trinity and he did not believe that Jesus died for his sins. He thought the classic northern baptism was having your bike stolen; he thought the classic Confirmation was when you got your first hickey. He also thought Grandma's bannock fresh out of the oven was his Communion.

He shakes his head thinking about this and, now, here he is: older, with his Granny talking and trusting him with stories about the old ways, about how a bear always knows what you're thinking, about how it's the dragonfly who can move through the four worlds. Her English is getting better as his Dogrib limps along. He's listening and sees she's been using her Bingo dabber to mark her days on the calendar. *What is she waiting for?* he wonders.

She is talking about how she used beaver castors to save his uncle's leg. How she cut each one into four under the full moon before doctoring him.

He's listening and wonders what he's missing tonight. There's a party at The Maze, for sure. *Maybe Juliet will be there, maybe not. She's already got eyes for Johnny,* he thinks. *I can't believe she and Darcy McMannus humped. How cheap. Darcy "McAnus"? What a lump!*

His Granny has twenty sheets out and he sees that she's offering him to play four, for luck. "*Nah,*" she says.

"*Ehtsi,*" he says. "I'm going out."

He's made her tea. She has her bannock and jam and butter. He's boiled three eggs for her and set aside salt and pepper, the big spoon for cracking, the knife for sawing and the little spoon for eating. He's boiled the eggs for four minutes exactly and now they're cooling in a bowl. She eats them cold with a pile of salt and pepper. She'll be fine tonight. He's made her a pot of tea, which she'll sip with a ton of sugar and cream from a can.

"*Nah*," she offers him her Bingo dabber again. "*Ho*."

"*In leh*," he says. "I gotta go, *Ehtsi*."

"Where?" she says. "To another party?"

He can't lie to her. "Granny, don't be like that. I'm young. I wanna go out."

"I dreamt of a white dragonfly last night," she says.

"Oh?" he asks. This is new.

"It's you," she says. "It's good luck. We'll win tonight. I can feel it."

"How?" Kevin asks. There's his coat. His shoes. He's got forty bucks. Enough to go Bazook.

"Itchy palms," she says and holds them up. "Come on, you. We'll split the jackpot and eat Cheezies."

Kevin grins. "*Ehtsi*," he says. "You keep it."

"Twenty grand," his Granny looks at him and beams.

"What?"

She nods. "They're raising money for the Handi Bus. Some *moonyow* crashed it and now they need a new door for the wheel-chair lift."

"Twenty grand," he says. "Seriously?"

She nods. "*Heh eh. Sombah cho.* We'll split it. Come you, my white dragonfly."

Twenty grand, Kevin thinks. *Ten thousand reasons to stay in*. He looks out the window and sees the cars and trucks whizzing by. *You can feel it*, Kevin thinks. *Friday night. This town loves to party and I can feel it.*

His Granny holds out her Bingo dabber to him. *She's lonely*, he thinks. *All her friends are gone.*

He goes to her, takes the Bingo dabber, kisses the top of her forehead and smiles. "Okay, Granny. I'll stay, but if I win, you have to let me buy you breakfast tomorrow at the café."

"Deal," she smiles.

Kevin sits beside her and touches her hand as he takes the Bingo dabber. *A white dragonfly, huh?* he thinks. *And ten grand? That's a lot of booze, a lot of pot. Maybe a truck. Maybe a trip to Edmonton, to West Ed. That's a lot of action. Maybe my new Amazement Plan starts tonight.*

"I love you, Granny," he says. "Even if we don't win."

"Oh we'll win. These itchy palms never lie. They were itchy the night I met Alphonse and they were itchy the night you were born." She wrinkles her nose at him and pushes him lightly. "You grew up so fast."

He looks at his four sheets as the local town station switches from Fort Simmer community announcements to the live broadcast of the Bingo. Kevin thinks about how he and the TV are his Granny's only friends. She turns it on first thing every day for company. She hardly goes out anymore and her only visitor now is the nurse, to check up on her.

Kevin's palms start to itch and burn and he looks at them, marvels at them.

"See?" his Granny says. "Feel them?"

He looks at his hands and then he looks at her. "Yes. Yes! I feel them."

"I told you," she says and smiles. "Good luck."

JOHNNY BECK IS in awe of his looks as he works out, and he loves the aroma of his own musk. It's the smell of his uncles after

143

they hunt and the memory of his father carrying him when he used to pretend to be asleep. Johnny's arms are tight after seven reps of preacher curls, and he loves how he looks in the mirror. He flexes and hears Donny stir and call for him in his sleep. Johnny makes sure his little brother is okay before taking another moment to admire himself in his mother's full-length mirror. *Is it my eyes? Is it my smile?* A thought hits him, a realization: *You know what I need?* he thinks. *I need an "in."* Someone to *get me closer to Juliet Hope, past the mugwumps. I need an apostle, so who's the sucker? Who's it gonna be?* Donny stirs again and Johnny watches, listens. *He's had way too much sugar tonight.* "I will do better tomorrow, buddy," he whispers. Johnny surveys his mother's bedroom. It's filthy. *What a pig*, he thinks. And all of a sudden it comes to him: Larry Sole. That lost little boy of a man who always sits alone and is always watching Juliet. *Yes, let it be him who gets me to her.* He catches his reflection in the mirror again and smiles. *Ladies*, he thinks. *It's not even fair what I have. Not. Even. Fair.*

DARCY MCMANNUS IS spinning. His thoughts are slow and looming as he watches the red glow of the hot knives die.

"Do you want me to?" Jazz asks.

"What?"

"Do you want me to?"

"No." He sits up—or tries to. He's so tired, so wasted, so done.

"You sure?"

"Yeah, don't."

"But it's fun."

"Don't," Darcy commands Jazz with his eyes, or tries to. *Who does Jazz think he is? There was a time I never had to repeat myself.*

"I'm gonna," Jazz says, rolling up his sleeve.

"What did I just say?" Darcy says again. *Who the eff does Jazz think he is? Since last summer, Jazz has become more cunning, more ...sinister.*

"Try and stop me," Jazz grins.

Darcy tries to stand but he's too stoned. He slurs something that sounds like it came from somebody behind him.

Jazz starts to giggle. Then he starts to bray.

The Jackal, Darcy thinks. *They call Jazz the Jackal because of that laugh. It's a half screech or half howl, like something wild and on fire running through the night.*

"I can't," Darcy wheezes. "I can't stand."

"That was more than a joint," Jazz says. "I put a little magic in there. A little—how you say—hibiscus?"

"What?" Darcy realizes. "What did we just smoke?"

Jazz reaches into the fish tank and grabs Fishy, the pregnant fish—Darcy's favourite. "Watch," he says.

"Don't!" Darcy reaches. He sees his own hand. It's meant for power and to punish and crush. Now it can only reach. He feels little. Jazz squeezes Fishy hard. Fishy explodes into a pink fleshy mist and hundreds of pink somethings are born through Jazz's fingers.

"I'm a god," Jazz says and roars with laughter. "I just made a million babies in my name. They were born through me and already sing my name."

Darcy focuses on what's left of the mother. Her mouth moves, gasping once. One of her eyes has pushed out sideways and is looking right at him.

"Jesus!" Darcy flushes and sinks into the couch. *I will never tell anyone about this, especially Juliet. What would she say? What would she think of me? Juliet, where are you?* he wonders. *Help me!*

"What you're thinking about, D?" Jazz asks as he examines his dripping hand. Things are moving between his fingers. Baby fish. They either have tails or long fins. "Hey. They tickle."

Darcy weaves. "When I get up—"

"What are you gonna do?" Jazz approaches him. "Here. Smell this."

Jazz smears his fingers all over and inside Darcy's nose and nostrils. Darcy's skull is filled with an ocean he's only seen in pictures and on TV. It's sweet and sour and his nostrils are moving. From the inside. Those babies—the living tissue of them—are inside his nose and crawling up!

Jazz scream-laughs in Darcy's face as Darcy pinches his nose to snuff it out. It's moving, wriggling, but he can't even lift his arms. He's stoned. Body stoned. And now sleepy. The baby fish are crawling up his nose: they're inside his skull.

He realizes he's crying, sobbing. *Why can't I move?*

Jazz flips the fish tank over, and the other fish Darcy loves spill onto the carpet. Jazz starts jumping up and down on each one as it tries to wriggle away. "Juliet was mine!" he screams. "She was supposed to be all mine!"

God, Darcy prays. *Get me out of here!*

LARRY SOLE HAS wings but only he can see them. *Wait. That's not true. Maybe Juliet can see them when she catches me watching her,* he thinks. *She watches me, too. I can feel it. She must know that I am the Ambassador of Love. I am a soldier of passion.* He is out past the highway, standing quietly in the middle of a dog team. Huskies. Some of them are half wolf. All of them are sleeping. He's slipped through them all. He's learned to put his spirit into the back pocket of his jeans so no one or nothing can sense him. Jed told him about how the Slavey used to be able to do this before battle and he's doing it now. *What is the new kid Johnny doing right now?* he wonders. *What is Juliet up to tonight? Or Darcy and Jazz—I wonder who's the most dangerous of them all?* The husky to his right stirs and quiets. *When will Jed come home? There was a trapper who came by an hour ago but it wasn't Jed. Jed's Tundra doesn't have a rifle rack. Mom's studying. I'll make her bannock when I go home. That always cheers her up. Oh, but then she'll see my tattoo.*

Larry had spent the afternoon drawing a love spell on his right hand: for Juliet Hope.

She will fall in love with me tonight, he thinks. She will. Even from this distance, this distance between us. It's shrinking. I know you can feel it, Juliet. With invisible ink and a raven feather, I have created love medicine for us. I have a triangle on my palm to show the three emotions you feel when you find love: faith, hope and attraction. There's a leaf with roots underneath the triangle because it represents growth, and I drew two hearts with a line joining them and that's a star above the triangle because it represents beauty. There's three throwing stars to defend us because this town loves to tear happy couples apart. There's a peace sign because we should feel peace when we're in love and there's a box coloured in because love is like winning Black Out Bingo when it's shared. There's a boomerang so our love will always come back stronger, and I drew a heart alone so if anyone tries to take Juliet away from me it won't work for them, and I drew an infinity circle and an amethyst to capture the light of the world and even the northern lights, and I drew a baby raven to honour the feather of this spell because I heard ravens can grow to be a hundred years old so our love will last a hundred years easy. Even if Juliet can't see my hand, I know she can feel it. Juliet, when you and I kiss, the night will explode into fire and angels. Even if I never have the chance to make love to you, I will always praise you. I will always adore you. I will always cherish you in everything I do from this moment on. You are the reason I was born. Where God's hands never went, I can reach that place for you. They say love is a thunder and I feel it in my everything for you. My love for you is so loud that it's practically bubonic. I raise my fist and swear it.

And that's when the huskies wake up.

How I Saved Christmas

Things to do today:
Get laid
Wake up Clarence
Make better friends with the BJs!
Go to dentist
Go to drum dance

Well, I'm just groovy. Believe it. I'm in shop right now, finishing off a ring. It's simple really, how it's done. You take a hollowed out aluminum rod and you saw off an inch from the end and you buff it, sand it, shine 'er up and that's it. The shop teacher, Koala Mercier, is a burn out. Mostly we just leave him alone cuz we know he's about three months away from his pension.

He says my ring is by far the best. I engraved "S.O.P." on the ring in cool gothic letters. "S.O.P" stands for "Soldier of Passion." The chalkboard reads: "ONLY 14 MORE WELDING DAYS BEFORE CHRISTMAS!" and I have to get out of this town: my moshing is at an all time high and my soul right now is a caved-in dog cage. But enough about me.

See, I'm writing lots these days and I'm really hoping it'll take me places. I hand all the finished products to my new English teacher, Mr. Ron, who truly believes in me. He says I should explore other media and that I got what it takes. Oh yeah, I should tell you: I got stabbed in the back as well. See, when I hand in my stories, they're pretty Barbara Psychedelica and I got assigned to a counselor. His name is Mr. Williams. He has pens and posters in his office that read, "THEY HAVEN'T BUILT AN AX THAT CAN CHOP DOWN A DREAM." He tries and all. I just can't get into it. He talks about Maslow's hierarchy of needs and priorities and setting goals while I look out the window to the far surrendered sky. It's sad really. But what can you do?

All I know is, I went into the bathroom, right outside his classroom and wrote on the wall "Last Chance For Doggy Style—200 Meters." And I signed it: "Mister Williams, Guidance Counselor Extrordinaire." Then I added: "God Bless the BJs!"

The new English teacher, Mr. Ron, says if I can do prose, a play, some poetry and fiction, I'll be able to get into this writing school down south. You'd swear my teacher has nocturnal emissions about my potential because he's already called and requested pamphlets. Here is an example of the poetry I've done so far:

Girls
Double jointed
Best spellers around
Always remember birth dates
Want to know your middle name!

Groovy, hey? That was written for this babe called Dedrie Meddows who has chrome submission tits. All I know is I ended up in Clarence's bathroom playing rock-paper-scissors with him for the best condoms. Clarence got the Crown and scored his first cousin. That was the night we were stoned on shrooms spitting apple juice at each other. It was sloppy lumberjack magic and I got to listen to Clarence's ass hydraulics slap his wet playdough balls off her ass for an hour. They sounded like this: slap! slap! slap!

When I fooled around with Dedrie, she kept asking, "What are you thinking? What are you thinking?"

I was just so amazed with her full, high, self-supporting breasts and hollow head nipples, I cried with delight: "Look at them biscuits! Look at them biscuits!"

"Don't make it dirty!" she cried back and pushed me away. And I, under the Jesus Cameras, could not perform.

"Go," she said. "Just go."

"Well could we spoon?" I asked. Banished, I ended up doing a black-out dance with a sock around my neck. An hour later, Lila showed up and I'm talking straight funkadelic.

So here's two little quickies that can sum up my winter so far:

Video Games
If you kill these men
you can touch this woman

Pornos
The gentle things
they shove into each other

Which reminds me. It's 3:30. Almost home time. I have to look at my list:

Things to do today:
Get laid
Wake up Clarence
Make better friends with the BJs!
Go to dentist
Go to drum dance

"Gentlemen!" Koala calls out from his office, "if your work stations are clean, you may leave!"

BRRRRRRRRRRRRRRRR!!

That's the buzzer. I grab my parky and pull on my Kamiks. It's time to wake up Clarence.

God really worked it out this year: Christmas is gonna be on a Sunday and New Year's Eve is gonna be on a Saturday. It's the coldest day of the year by the way: minus 45 degrees. That's not including wind or A-hole factor. You may have heard of the SAD syndrome. I think it's "Sloppy Lumberjacks and Depression" or somethin', but what it boils down to is a lack of light: Death by darkness. We are humans but we are also plants, and if a plant cannot get enough light, it cannot grow. Simple. When humans can't get enough light, they swallow shotgun barrels and pull triggers. That's my buddy Clarence if I'm not careful.

The good thing about it being minus 45 degrees is that the sunrise is spectacular. It's a Physics 30 orgasm. The light from the sun, which is low to the horizon, hits the ice-fog which hangs over this little northern town and you have rarefaction, refraction and some fancy light that makes you ache. Too bad you can't enjoy it without your cheeks splitting, it's that cold. And you would not bleed blood, either. You would bleed purple purple steam.

And something else: the snow here is as white as the milk of apples and the trees look like snapshot explosions. Wow, hey?

Dogs

Let's talk about 'em! I finally figured out why they're on this planet. They are the Jesus Cameras. What they see, Jesus and all the angels see. If you're smoking up with Nostradamus, for example, he'd be quite a party pooper. He'd be droning on and on a little like this:

NOSTRADAMUS: "You guys are dead. You're so dead.

Millenium, baby. Get ready. Bombs. Fire. Cannibals. Cockroaches. One from the lesser tribes will acquire arms and toast your ass."

ME (AMBASSADOR OF LOVE): "Hey, Nos, quit hogging the hooka and shut your mouth, bee-otch!"

Anyways, the point is that if you were smoking up and you

were on parole and a dog was in the room, it would really be Jesus and all the angels watching. That's the scoop, Jupe! And cats are Devil Cameras; they're Satan's little helpers. From their eyes, Satan and all his minions watch with drooling lips. And now you know why dogs and cats hate each other. The light and darkness war continues!

The BJS

I guess I should divulge the best kept secret in Simmer: The Blow Job Specialist! I don't know where she learned her oral techniques, but I sat at the base of Clarence's steps one night listening to him get a "Cosmic Blowjob" (his words) from her. I don't know if she took both of his jobbles in her mouth and sucked at the same time; I don't know if she stroked his prostate with her longest finger; I don't know what she did but he was wailing like a horse lit on fire. He still can't talk about what she did without twitches and spasms. All I know is he slept for days after and the BJS had vanished long before he woke up.

She isn't the prettiest girl in town, and I think that's why she had to go beyond the norm. Who taught her? Porn? Who?

Eight months black for slaves

Did I tell you I woke up to the sound of sizzling hash between the blades of squeezing knives? My Uncle Franky, a good man with a dependency problem, was hooting away and rolling fatties. No breakfast! Not even coffee! Just some black hash for a broken god seeking collision.

"Mornin'," I said as I got up and jumped into some long johns. "Howshegoin?"

"Pretty purple," my uncle said, meaning "hazy." "Jed and I were up 'til two last night making Grizzly patties for this catering gig he got for the drum dance."

I watched Uncle Frank brace for the smoke.

"Wanna know what?" He hooted. "Clarence (hoot) lost his birthday money to Tarvis last (hoot) night (hoot) at the bar."

"Fuck sakes," I said. "That damn Clarence."

Before I was out the door, my Uncle coughed, "Sal Bright (hoot hoot) don't wanna be Santa no more!"

But I didn't listen. I had to get my sweet ass to school.

Clarence

Now let's take a look at how the eight month winter of the NWT affects mammals. Let's start off with Clarence Jarome who I have known since I moved here. After I lost rock-paper-scissors to him for the Crown condom, we kind of looked at this little bottle of baby oil on the sink, and I asked, "Well, should we play for it?"

Hell yes! We played best out of three and I lost, I lost, I lost. That party was absolute monkey house trauma. We had Slayer, D.R.I., Monster Magnet and Danzig on CD shuffle. I was a sunshine cannibal moshing it up in my toque and mukluks.

"I didn't know you were a thrasher," Lila smiled, standing there in her bizarre purple sweater and her sweet little ABBA shoes. I danced, sized her up, looked into her mouth and thought YES!

Clarence yelled. "Play Slayer's 'Mandatory Suicide'!"

Oh how we moshed. No Pink Floyd please. No Jimmy H. Just some kick ass hard core. To make a long story short: I had to stickhandle around Lila's Jackie Chan boyfriend who was selling "White Widow" out of his I-ROC. He left to make the deal of the century and I took full hunger advantage. Slap, slap, slap…

This was a great year for the alternative lifestyle by the way: Great porn courtesy of Andrew Blake, great music courtesy of Napster, and I've just made friends with the BJS.

But enough about that. Let's get back to the quest.

Clarence had a tape of mine, which I stole off Eric. Eric and

Clarence aren't speaking to each other anymore cuz Clarence puked on Eric's back. Such is life!

Here's who Eric puts on his tapes: The Cranes, The Prodigy, Afghan Whigs, Dead Can Dance, Slowdive, Siouxsie and the Banshees, Kate Bush, Jonathan Richman and The Modern Lovers. The best the best the best!

He calls this tape "The Grinder" and I'll need it as I nurture the sacred bond between the BJs and *moi*.

Anyways, I ran over to Clarence Manor cuz I'm his human alarm clock. He's kind of depressed lately and Prozac lets him sleep fourteen hours straight. It was his birthday yesterday. It even said so on the green screen. His house is across the potato field and I froze my ass off—even with added protection like woollies and long johns. I pulled my toque all the away down so I could see through the wool mesh and still I froze. Nobody on the streets but me. No parka queens to wave to. Eyes so cold they water. Snow piled high like thick, white mattresses, burying the hoods of trucks. It's like walking into a frozen marshmallow. Everything outside was so suddenly still and the air hung like a pregnant moose. One false move and the trees would shatter.

There was Clarence's house. I let myself in.

Clarence, as usual, was in his coma deep sleep. He's on pogey and doesn't have to work.

"Mono Boy!" I called as I barreled up the stairs. No answer, the chronic. Man, I swear Clarence was born tired.

"Lost your money last night, hey?" I threw his gonchies from the floor to his face.

"What!" Clarence sat up. "How the hell do people know these things?"

"Just do, now where's my tape—what the...?"

Something had changed about his room. It was still a mess with his CDs and tapes piled all over the place. He had posters up of Morrissey, The Cure and The Smiths. There were also pictures of Bat Girl all over the place with loving attention on her latex ass. His laundry basket was overflowing and my porno mags were fanned out all over his floor. What the hell? There were bullet holes in the walls!

There were about 20 bullet holes peppered all over the far walls and ceiling. It was his .22 caliber AR-7 survival rifle that he cradled in his arms. He had his banana clip, which meant he was capable of 33 semi-automatic shots as fast as he could pull the trigger. I won't go hunting anymore with him because of that gun.

"I thought you sold that," I said.

He looked at me. "Your tape is on the top shelf, by the shotgun. Now who the hell told you?"

"Clarence," I said, "what the hell happened here last night?"

"Spiders. I hear them in the walls."

I stared at him, hard.

"I know I know. I gotta get outta this town."

I looked for my tape. He pulled on his Sisters of Mercy T-shirt. "I swear to God this house is haunted. I gotta get out of here."

I found the tape. "Gretzky!" I put it in his ghetto and played it. It was Jonathan Richman and the Modern Lovers: "I go to bakeries all day long; there's a lack of sweetness in my life…"

"Lare!" he ran his hands through his hair. "Last night I turned 21. It's almost Christmas. I looked around, I looked at my friends and I just wanted to cry. I gotta get a job. I miss it. Oh God, I miss working."

I turned it down. "Give it time."

"Time? I don't got time! You know how close I came to pulling the trigger last night?"

I stuck my finger in one of the bullet holes. "Not worth it, man. Besides, who will the spiders play with?"

"I walked around the bar," he continued. "Yelling across the tables made me deaf, so I danced on the floor all by myself. I looked at the moose and caribou heads above the bar with their mouths open. I just walked up to them and said I was sorry. Somebody stuck red pool balls in the eye sockets of the buffalo skulls. I saw all the fish mounted on the walls, those big pikes and whitefish. I just walked up and said I was sorry. I poured beer in their mouths and got kicked out. On my birthday! It's Christmas for chrissakes." He paused. "I seen Sal Bright there. He don't wanna be Santa anymore."

"Look," I held out my hand. "We're making a deal right now. We won't deal with lotteries under 30 million."

"30 million!"

"Yeah," I grinned, "cuz we're worth it."

"Can't do it, man. There's a bingo in Hay River next week."

"Clarence," I said, "God won't give us this forever."

"What?"

"God gave us today and I'm gonna use it. I'm going. Don't forget about the drum dance tonight."

"Where?"

"Friendship Centre. Eight o'clock."

"Let's have a coffee," he said. "Then we'll play crib."

"No time, partner!" I said. "I got my tape, now I gotta see Eichman!"

"Eichman? Jesus! Isn't he secretly the lead singer for Rammstein? Hey! Don't you wanna hear how I lost my birthday money?"

"Naw," I got up. "You did it last year and you'll probably do it again next year—"

"But, Larry!"

"Sol later, man!" I yelled. "Happy Birthday!"

That's what I did in front of the Jesus Cameras and everyone: Tough love, baby!

"I deserve to be loved by a beautiful and intelligent woman," I said to myself as I made a break for it. "I deserve to be loved by a beautiful and intelligent woman."

It was so cold out I cut through the old folk's home. Here the elders had all this tinsel and Christmas propaganda happening around them and they looked sad. Some of them were reading the paper and shaking their heads. Man, the old people in this town smoke like chimneys. Crazy coots!

On to Eichman

I gotta tell you about the dentist here. He's cold: a true technician of terror and torture. He's the type of guy who probably laughed when Old Yeller took a bullet in the head. Anyways, I walked into his chop shop and somebody had been hard at'er decorating the place for Christmas. There was music coming from the office and, sure enough, it was Boney M singing "Faleece Navee Datt!!" Along with the punishing sound of a drill from the operating room, there was a coffee machine hissing out a fresh pot. There were charts all over the wall saying, "Gum Disease: prevention is the key."

The whole place smelled like cinnamon slaughter. There was a pile of *Reader's Digests* in a pile on a coffee table. I sat down on the couch. Over to the far left, under the coat rack, and beside the coffee machine, was a pair of white Kamiks standing in a puddle. Above them were parkas and a pair of big-ass caribou mitts. There was this little kid there, looking at me. Beside him sat his dad. The kid was reading a book. I poured a cup. My hands were a bruised purple. I'm surprised they just didn't seize. There was the latest *Slave River Journal* and the cover reported: "Sal Bright will no longer be Santa!"

What the!?—I picked it up and read it.

His quote: "Due to the politics, I cannot remain true to the cause. If I spend too much time in Indian Village, the Metis get mad at me; if I spend too much time near the church, the Dene get mad; if I don't spread myself around, the non-Natives get mad and that isn't what Christmas is about. Besides, why not have someone else give it a try?"

The article went on and on. I couldn't believe it. That's what my uncle and Clarence were talking about. That's why the elders were shaking their heads and looking sad. I was going to steal the article to read later but a woman came out of the operating room looking pale and wobbly. Half her face was falling off by the look of it.

"Hullo," I said and took off my jacket.

"Honey," the father greeted.

"Mum, can I have some ice cream?" the little guy asked.

She said, "Asha Ukka Ukka!"

Her face was so frozen!

"Are you okay? Here's your jacket." Her husband said. She looked wasted. From behind her came Eichman himself. "Next week, Barbara. Ten o'clock, Tuesday?"

Barbara turned around and floppily waved at him, kind of groggy like, and kept rambling, "Alsha Ulsha Uka Uka."

The family left. Eichman stared after them, smiling. I could hear his assistant washing up for me. I heard from the scurvy dogs in the high school that she was a sweet little honey who didn't drink or go out at all. The first week she got here, the meat hooks were out. Guys got all dressed up and cruised in their trucks doing a smoke show at the four-way by spinning out. When she went to do her shopping at the Bay, all the packing boys tripped on their dicks rushing to be the one to pack for her. Clarence said the boys were being shot down on all fronts and they were too devastated to call a retreat. And now I'd have my moment in the sun—with what? A damn drill in my mouth and a needle sliding through my gums.

"Larry Sole?" she called out. Eichman was still staring off as Barbara and her fam wobbled through the snow.

"*C'est moi*," I said and hung up my jacket.

First I saw the hair, then her bust which heaved like war cannons under her lily white suit. What a presence! I looked at her slim trim tummy and bet she had a six pack. I sat down on the seat. Sure I did. It had this rattly white paper that wrinkled and crackled whenever I moved. I was getting settled when she came from the office with a file. Wow! A brunette with straight hair tied in a bun. She was trying to be professional and all by tying this bib around me, but she had to lean her chest near my face and I wanted to snap my teeth and hang on like a wolverine.

Eichman came in and looked at a file she handed him. I leaned over and checked out the feet. Moccasins! The beadwork didn't look Dogrib, Slavey or Chipewyan. Where was she from?

Eichman perused my file, probably plotting the best routes for attack and carnage. Ever since I can remember, Eichman had this one poster on the damn ceiling. It's this witch with a warty nose and most of her teeth are missing. The tooth stubs she does have left are black and yellow. She's green and spooky and she's holding a lollypop as big as your ass. She's asking, "Care for some candy, my sweet?"

And in the back of her, there's more candy and mountains of lollypops. I remember we were talking one day at school, me and the boys. We all agreed this poster has created more nightmares, more trauma, more scorched shorts than *The Exorcist*. I mean, what kind of sick bastard puts up that kind of poster for children, elders and expecting moms to look at while he solders their teeth shut or slices into their gums?

"When was your last checkup?" Eichman asked.

"Six months ago," I lied.

"Bite on this," he said and put something in my mouth that bit with plastic teeth into my gums. He aimed a magnificent rifle at my face, near my cheek and I checked out the Dene honey as she put this heavy blanky on me. A heart shaped ass. Sweet! Sweet!

The blanky was lead insulated, I guess, with a big flap meant for genitalia. The way she was putting it on was like she was tucking me in and I was tempted to say, "Night, Mommy," but, instead, being Big Daddy Love and all, I leaned forward and sniffed her hair and she smelt like something blue and lush and bright, like the water children are baptized with.

"Where you're from?" I asked.

"Hold still!" Eichman ordered and felt my cheeks.

"Deline'," she said darting her eyes between Eichman and I. Nervous, I guess, cuz she was working.

"You know Jed?" I asked. He was from Franklin.

"Jed!" she beamed, "Yes I do! Where is he?"

"Cember, please," Eichman said, meaning "Shut up," and to me: "Will you hold still?"

"He's going out with my mom. He'll be at the drum dance tonight. He's doing the catering."

Eichman man-handled me into silence. Can you believe it? What a power freak. There was the crinkle of the paper beneath me, and my feet were getting hot as I still had on my boots and woollies. The scent of a cinnamon death soaked into my clothes and skin, suffocating the small mouths of my pores. He and Cember left the room. I heard, "Clear" and the magnificent rifle went "Brr" and that was it. I looked up to the old hag with the crumbling teeth gurgling. "Care for some candy, my sweet?"

"Open," Eichman said and held out his white-gloved hand. With my white froth cow tongue, I pushed it out and there was a stringy slug trail of spit, which he lassoed around the plastic blade. He handed it to Cember who took it and left the room. He put the plastic blade on the other side and did the whole process again.

I stared into the mouth of the hag on the ceiling and plotted erogenous camera mischief: (Me, Cember: slap! slap! slap!)

When Eichman and Cember were finished, they whispered tiny black secrets back and forth. I started thinking about Sal Bright, Simmer's Santa. He just had to be Santa this year. For as long as I can remember, he would always dress up and have his wife pull him on a sleigh with their car. He'd crank up a huge generator for the thousands of lights and blaring music to announce Santa's arrival on your street. It was like the hand of God when he appeared. The lights, the music, the magic of it all with him waving and smiling.

You could always hear him "HO HO HO'ing" all over town through his megaphone and the dogs would howl and chase him like some parade of beast demons trying to tear a holy man down. Kids would all run up to their windows and wave like convicts. Even parents shoveling their driveways would wipe their runny noses on the back of their woolly mitts and smile.

If he wasn't Santa this year, the whole damn thing wouldn't work. I knew it. Even if I was a preaching hypocrite most of the time and even if there would always be a "Care for some candy, my sweet?" poster up in the dentist's office, you just had to have Christmas to stretch out and wiggle your toes. There were 2,500 of us humans here in Simmer and the year had been so hard with all the lay-offs and cutbacks.

Eichman stood above me. Cember sat beside me. He was gabbing on and on: "...cap has fallen out and we'll put it back on for you."

I guess I was thinking so hard I didn't notice Eichman was

already greasing up a Q-tip with some paste and squeezing my cheeks together so I'd open up.

"We've also found a small cavity on your..."

"Aw who cares," I thought. "Do your job, eh? You're going to hurt me either way."

It never failed. Every time I came in, I knew I was gonna suffer. Eichman never failed to incinerate my central nervous system with a blade or needle. He swabbed my lower back gum and I looked at Cember.

"If anything happens, baby," I wanted to say, "tell 'em I cared. Tell 'em I was a bright light in a two dollar town."

So I took notes of everything that went on in my head while they drilled, sucked and needled my teeth and gums. Here it is and it's important that I document how the government and the dentists are taking out the Soldiers of Passion: I'm not going to change a damn word. You deserve the pure octane, unadulterated, calligraphy-on-Wednesdays truth. Here it is: "FASCIST ROOT KILLER! I HAVE THE HUGE WHITE EYES OF BISON BEFORE THE BULLET SPLITS THE SKULL THEY MIGHT AS WELL BE STICKING A BARREL IN MY MOUTH I CAN'T IT'S NOT NO FROZEN HURTS HURTS HURTS I'M A RATTLESNAKE MY VENOM HE'S TRYING TO GET AT THE MAIN TRUNK NERVES THAT HAVE FUNNELED AND TUNNELED INTO THE ROOT SYSTEM OF MY FACE OH JESUS JESUS PLUCK ME YOUR BRIGHTEST FLOWER FROM THIS YOUR TRAUMA GARDEN MY TONGUE THE NEEDLE COULD TAKE YOU SO EASILY STINKY GLOVES NOW I'M DELIRIOUS TEN YEARS OF THERAPY AND I MIGHT JUST MAKE IT I'M GURGLING BLOOD PLEASE STOP PLEASE STOP THE WHITE PAIN FROM MY MOUTH EXPLODES BUTTERFLY SNOW FROM IT FALLS I'M..."

"Care for some candy, my sweet?"

All done. They wiped their hands of cold medical slaughter. I needed some water to gurgle the spit and blood. "Who," I thought, "who has placed a burning stalk of rhubarb in my mouth?"

Eichman beamed. "You had quite the little nap."

Cember undid my bib and looked at me with her teardrop eyes.

"I deserve to be loved by a beautiful and intelligent woman," I tried to say but alls that came out was: "Alsha alsha uka aka."

"Eeeeeezzzzzyyy," she helped me get up. I wobbled out of the room and there was somebody else waiting.

Floppily, I got my coat. Floppily, I looked at Cember and wove a little kiss, which I summoned from my dry throat, past my swollen moose lips, through my teeth towards her. But she looked away and was on to other things.

"Too bad, baby," I thought, "we coulda' been good together..."

I practically fell down the stairs I was so weak. I pulled on my mitts and toque. "Wait a minute," I thought. "Wait one rattle-snake minute."

I turned around. Eichman was staring at me through his window, smiling.

I got the hell away.

I guess while me and my moose lips are walking home, and while I'm having my ears stung by a thousand invisible snow bees, I should tell you about me trying to get laid all the time. I'm really quite reckless about my sexuality, and I'm ready to rock any day of the week, but that's only because I'm a product of a lonely town. I mean this town is full of flatliners. A soul hits the ground here every seven seconds.

I realized last Tuesday how lonely I was and it hit me. Hard. So I put some condoms by my bed and I gave all my porno mags to Clarence. Some people have to walk off hangovers or bouts of fury; I have to walk off The Heat. With leather suit shoes through knee high snow, I walk, patrol and search, led by the heavy eyes of hunger, looking for love. Damn this sexual peak! Damn it straight to hell!

This town. Home of the big diesels, big track pants and big bad booze faces. I know every inch of this cage and it's only getting smaller—and I refuse to play Bingo! Don't even get me started about Bingo. I want to kill that game! And come to think of it, when was the last time a woman seduced me? When was the last time someone spent hours plotting how to get me into the sack? When was the last time someone came up to me and said, "Larry, I think you're funnier than a French tickler! I think you're the only one who hasn't been on empty for the past three years!"

I mean, these topics have to be addressed.

And I'm a good lay. I'm officially a good lay. After all, my blood is loaded with Testosterone making my balls 340 twin overhead cams jacked to the nuts!

And this town doesn't help. They take with their teeth here. There should be a sign on the airport road that reads:

WELCOME TO FORT SIMMER

PUMPIN' CAPITAL OF THE NWT

IF WE CAN'T KNOCK YOU UP WE'LL KNOCK YOU OUT!

And when you leave this little hellhole, there should be a sign on the highway that says:

THANK YOU FOR VISITING

COME AGAIN

IF WE COULDN'T BREED YOU WE PROBABLY BEAT YOU!

Yes, yes, they may have labeled me a failure in physics; they may have called home because I have four lates, but they did not see me for the gift of spirit and breath that I am.

I went home. It was my turn to cook and I couldn't wait until the drum dance to eat. I wrote one outstanding poem thinking about the Old Folk's Home. It went like this:

The Breath Of Elders
The breath of elders
like the breath of elephants close
fear mouse and his dream
for mouse has the dream of flight above snow
and mouse has the nightmare of teeth and steel
and steel is the cage of dog
and dog is chained
dog wants pussy
pussy is eating its cold bald litter
and the litter bald has the dream of nipples
and nipples love the taste of teeth
and teeth are the embrace for cannibals
and cannibals have to eat their buddies
and buddies never talk of love
and love is a porno with the sound turned low
and low is the swoop from hawk to mouse
and earth has risen to taste rain's skin
as skin is a field of dying flowers
and flowers are felt like God's fine hands
as he steals and holds the breath of elders...

After I finished, I just sat in the hallway with my purple ears defrosting from the sting of invisible snow bees. As the windows fogged up, I could smell the caribou hamburger sizzling in its sauce and in ten minutes the spaghetti would be ready. I kept thinking about passion, about how it was the last clean thing I had. I started thinking about how horribly pathetic this year would die if Sal Bright didn't play Santa. What about the kids? What about the elders? What about guys like Clarence or Uncle Frank? What about the community? What about the government workers? Any minute, something in their backs could blow. Even Eichman, what about him? I thought of all the seized metal engines outside and the seized human engines inside. And I thought of me. I needed it, too. I guess I had a grand mal seizure about the whole thing and decided it was up to me. I mean, didn't sometimes…didn't you ever think that you were dead, that you were already buried, but you were given one day to come back and make things right? One day—through the politics, lies and the sloppy lumberjack butchery, God's permission was yours to come back to bring light to the world and add another color to the rainbow?

No bullshit. This is how I saved Christmas on the coldest day of the year. I called Sal Bright up.

"Lo!" He called as he answered the phone.

"Hello, is this Sal Bright of Fort Simmer, Northwest Territories?"

"Yes it is."

"Sal, my name is Tarvis Marvin calling from Emmunton, Alberta."

"Zat right, eh?"

"Yes, Sir, and I represent the Canadian Council of Moments."

"The what?"

"Canadian Council of Moments. It's an international organization to honor and commemorate Soldiers of Passion."

"Izzat right?"

"Yessir, and, Sir, it is my sincere pleasure to award you with the Canadian Council of Moments Award."

"Oh?"

"Yessir and your name has also been put into this year's awards as well for your involvement as Santa Claus."

"Well," he breathed, "we might have a problem—"

"Sir," I interrupted, "I understand you are thinking of not being Santa this year."

"Yeah," he began, "see, we got so much politics here."

"I read."

"You did?"

"Yessir. We have eyes in the most unique places and we understand your feelings on this matter. That is why I decided to call you up myself and ask you—*no*—beg you to keep up the good work."

"Wow…"

"Yessir, we here at the Canadian Council of Moments have applauded your efforts from the very beginning and we are all holding our breath that you continue."

"Really?"

"Yessir, I want to tell you that you'll be receiving something very special in the mail."

"Oh?"

"Yes! A customized ring just for you that boasts 'S.O.P' for 'Soldier of Passion' and a thank you note from myself representing the council."

"Hey that's great!"

"You've earned it, Sir."

"Yeah, well, I guess I should tell you that it sure is wonderful being Santa."

"I bet!"

"Yeah, you see the kids and you see them waving and you know they might not get a thing for Christmas but you gave them this. You gave them something. I sure am glad you called," he continued. "I was thinking of taking the wife and kids up to Yellowknife for a break, but I think I'll stay. I just wish there wasn't politics."

"We know," I said. "We're only too aware of the situation and we sympathize with you."

"Thanks," he said. "Thanks a lot."

"So you'll do it?" I asked. "You'll be Santa?"

"Yes," he said. "Yes I will."

"Mahsi cho!" I yelled. "Woo hoo! You'll get your ring in the mail, Sir. And we'll be watching you this Christmas!"

"You bet!" He yelled. "Hey, honey! Hey, kids! I'm gonna be Santa again!" and I heard a cheer from his family.

And I heard a cheer from me. I had found another Soldier of Passion. And that, dear brothers and sisters, is how I saved Christmas.

O-lay!

Acknowledgements

THE AUTHOR WISHES to thank the Yellowknife Rotary Club, the Government of the Northwest Territories Student Services Department, the NWT Literacy Council, the Ontario Arts Council, Arctic College, the En'owkin Centre and the University of Victoria for their generous support.

Mahsi

THE ORIGINAL MUSIC score behind "The Monkeys of India" was provided by Peter Lauterman. Mahsi cho! Mahsi to Keith Smith for his rendition of "Child in Flames." Mahsi to Trevor Cameron and Ryan Klaschinsky for many odd and hilarious seeds. Mahsi to Lorne Simon for editing, inspiration and believing in me. I miss you. Mahsi to the Fields of the Nephilim for inspiring the novel's title with their song "Celebrate" off their *The Nephilim* album.

Mahsi to Barbara Pulling, Carolyn Swayze, Roger Brunt, Dylan Vasas, Moira Jones and Alec Lyne for their hawk-eyed editing and comments. Mahsi also to Trevor Evans, Mike, Jon Liv Jaque, James "Alien Autopsy" Croizier, Garth Prosper, Ms. Kelly Kitchen, Ron Klassen, Jason, Sarah Hodgkins, Junior Mercredi, Denise Williams, Clinton, Louise and Mike Spencer; also to anyone who's ever had anything to do with P.W.K. High School and Fort Smith, NWT. Mahsi to my brothers, Roger, Johnny and Jamie, for their inspiration and humour. Mahsi to my mom. Mahsi to my father. Mahsi also to each and every member of the Dogrib Nation of the Northwest Territories for their stories and power. Mahsi to the Creator for this my breath and eyes. Mahsi. Mahsi to the children of the world for their inspiration and innocence.

The writing here was inspired by the music and talent of The Cure, My Bloody Valentine, The Sisters of Mercy, Skinny Puppy, the *T2* Soundtrack, The Smiths, The Ministry, The Cocteau Twins, Kate Bush, Slowdive, Nick Cave, Dead Can Dance, The Mission, Iron Maiden and Fields of the Nephilim. Mahsi cho!